"I'm not your secretary, Joss!"

Kate's voice betrayed her anger. "There's no need to pander to my vanity by pretending you see me as a physically desirable woman."

As they neared the conservatory, Joss put his hand on her arm to stop her.

"What makes you think that I don't?" he asked her dispassionately. "Kate, if you're so convinced that at thirty-seven you're no longer a desirable, sensual woman, I can only think that you must consider me at forty-two to be past all hope."

"Don't be ridiculous," she told him sharply. "It's different for a man."

"Not these days," he returned equably. "Do you really consider yourself so old that no man could possibly find you desirable, or is that assumption a convenient self-delusion to hide behind?"

PENNY JORDAN was constantly in trouble in school because of her inability to stop daydreaming—especially during French lessons. In her teens she was an avid romance reader, although it didn't occur to her to try writing one herself until she was older. "My first half-dozen attempts ended up ingloriously," she remembers, "but I persevered, and one manuscript was finished." She plucked up the courage to send it to a publisher, convinced her book would be rejected. It wasn't, and the rest is history. Penny is married and lives in Cheshire.

Penny Jordan's striking mainstream novel, *Power Play*, quickly became a *New York Times* bestseller.

Books by Penny Jordan

PENNY JORDAN

a rekindled passion

Harlequin Books

TORONTO • NEW YORK • LONDON
AMSTERDAM • PARIS • SYDNEY • HAMBURG
STOCKHOLM • ATHENS • TOKYO • MILAN

Harlequin Presents first edition December 1990
ISBN 0-373-11324-2

Original hardcover edition published in 1989
by Mills & Boon Limited

CHAPTER ONE

'ALL ready for the wedding tomorrow, are you? What time is she getting married?'

Kate shook her head wryly in answer to the first part of the postman's question and offered, 'Half-past three,' to the second.

As she collected the unusually thick pile of envelopes from him with the warm smile that transformed the serious repose of her small, heart-shaped face, she wondered how long it would take her daughter to drive up from London. Sophy had promised to set off early so that they would have at least a couple of hours to catch up on one another's news before they started going through all the arrangements for tomorrow.

It hadn't been easy: organising the wedding for her daughter and her son-in-law-to-be, with both of them so busy in their careers that she hadn't even seen Sophy since the announcement of her engagement at Christmas, apart from one brief occasion just after Easter when she had gone to spend a few days with Sophy at John's family home in the south of England, at their invitation.

She had been dreading the visit, even though Sophy had assured her that John's parents were looking forward to meeting her, and had confirmed that she had told them everything.

That had been a hard decision for her to make, but she had felt that she owed it to Sophy to permit her to tell her in-laws-to-be the truth.

After the visit she was glad she had done so. John's parents had turned out to be a very pleasant and understanding couple in their late fifties. John was the youngest of their brood of four children, and Mary Broderick had had the same kind of briskly maternal warmth that Kate remembered from her own mother... and still missed.

How her mother would have enjoyed tomorrow. She had adored her only granddaughter...both her parents had, and she still missed them dreadfully, even though it was now nearly eight years since the plane crash that had taken their lives.

They had been marvellous parents, so understanding, so loving and protective of both her and Sophy. As she stood in her comfortable if rather shabby kitchen, she felt the hot burn of tears stinging the back of her eyes and grimaced to herself. She was thirty-seven years old, for heaven's sake... far too old to indulge in a silly bout of weeping, even if tomorrow she *was* going to have to close the door on a very precious period of her life.

Sophy, married... She grinned a little to herself, her mood changing. At nineteen Sophy had been a dedicated career woman, swearing that marriage for her was something she would not even contemplate until she was close to thirty, and yet here she was at twenty, going on twenty-one, fathoms deep in love; insisting that she was married traditionally from her childhood home in the small village church, surrounded by the people she had grown up among in an environment totally different from the fast pace of her London life.

Sophy was a thoroughly modern young woman, highly qualified and skilled, independent, ambitious and very mature. Kate loved her dearly, but from the day that Sophy left home to go to university she had fought desperately to give her her freedom . . . not to cling or be possessive about her, even though at first she had missed her desperately.

They had always been so close, and had stayed close despite the fact that Sophy now lived and worked in London, but from now on their relationship would be different . . . must be different. From now on, Sophy's first loyalty must be to the man she was marrying tomorrow.

Kate liked John, and would have liked him as a person even if he had not been deeply in love with her precious daughter.

She liked his family, too . . . liked their warmth and closeness, liked the way they were making Sophy welcome into that family . . . and she was grateful to them for their compassion in so calmly accepting the history of Sophy's conception and birth.

It must have come as quite a shock to them to learn that their son was marrying Sophy, a girl whose mother had conceived her when she was barely sixteen and unmarried; she knew, had their positions been reversed and *she* been the one to discover that her child was marrying someone whose mother had been sixteen and unmarried when she conceived, that she would have had serious doubts

as to both the emotional and moral stability of the
parenting that child had received.

Perhaps because of her own bitterly painful experience, she was very much aware that it took more
to lay the foundations for a marriage that would
hopefully be both loving and lasting than the ex-
citing but sometimes short-lived intensity of
physical and emotional desire. Things like mutual
trust and respect...backgrounds and beliefs that
meshed and sat easily within one another...a shared
sense of humour and purpose.

Sophy was a very sensible young woman, everything any mother could want in a daughter, and
Kate considered herself to have been unfairly
blessed in the gift of a daughter who had brought
her so much joy—as though fate had relented of
its earlier cruelty.

From the kitchen window she could see the men
hard at work in the garden erecting the marquee
which was to hold tomorrow's wedding guests, and
she reminded herself that now was not the time to
stand around daydreaming.

She flicked through the post...most of it was
cards for Sophy and John. She put these to one
side, on the old pine dresser which her parents had
inherited from her grandmother and she from them.

Its wood gleamed softly with the polish of generations, the thick willow-patterned pottery setting
off both the dark wood and the sunny yellow décor
of her kitchen.

She had lived in this house all her life, had grown
up here in this small Dales village where the people,
despite the outward apparent dourness, had, as she

had good reason to know, a warmth of heart and spirit that they gave generously to those they called their own.

There were Setons scattered all over this part of the world, the name originally belonging to a border family who had gradually spread southwards into the Dales.

Her grandfather had been a hill farmer, farming a land which had been in their family for generations. After his death, her father had sold the farm. It was small and unproductive and, as a lecturer at York University, he had not been in a position to concentrate on his career and to run the farm.

Kate hadn't gone to university. She *had* intended to do so... *had* had her career all mapped out: university, a degree and then a job teaching. Only it hadn't worked out like that. At sixteen, having just completed her O levels, she had gone south to Cornwall to spend a month's holiday with an aunt of her mother's who had just retired from nursing on the south coast, and it had been while she was there...

A battered Range Rover pulled up in front of the kitchen window, scattering gravel. Its driver, a tall, lithe redhead, got out as quickly and impulsively as she did everything else and came hurrying towards the back door.

'Hi... how's it going?' she demanded breathlessly, as she came in. 'What time does Sophy arrive?'

'I'm not sure. She said she'd try and make an early start. Coffee?' Kate invited, smiling at her best friend and business partner.

Lucy Grainger and her accountant husband had moved to the village ten years ago. Kate had met Lucy initially when both she and Lucy had literally bumped into one another outside the Post Office.

On first seeing Kate and Sophy together, Lucy had made the mistake that strangers inevitably made of thinking that she and Sophy were sisters and not mother and daughter. With only sixteen years between them, and with Kate being petite and so very youthful for her thirty-seven years that people thought she was in her late twenties and not her mid-thirties, it was a natural enough mistake, but one that still made Kate wince a little.

When Sophy had innocently called her Mummy she had braced herself for the familiar speculative look, but instead Lucy had simply said ruefully, 'Oh, dear, trust me... I've put my foot in it again.' And with the self-critical comment had come a look not of pity but of compassion and such understanding that Kate had found herself uncurling from her protective shell and responding to the warm friendship that Lucy offered her.

It had been just over seven years ago, soon after her parents' death, that Lucy had suggested that they combine their culinary talents and set up a small business catering for everything from weddings to dinner parties.

Egged on by Sophy, Kate had reluctantly agreed. The business had been a greater success than she had ever imagined, giving her not just more financial independence than she had ever expected to have, but also a new and thriving interest in life.

All through her pregnancy and Sophy's growing years she had deliberately kept to the quiet backwater of life, deliberately seeking its protective camouflage, and now, with Sophy's and Lucy's combined exhortations, she was finding that more exhilarating waters were nothing like so threatening as she had imagined.

Sophy, who knew her well, had challenged her initially when she had flatly refused to countenance Lucy's suggestion, saying firmly, 'Oh come on, Mama. Don't think I don't know what's behind this. You're out of date,' she told her ruthlessly. 'Or rather in the height of fashion,' she had added mischievously, watching with a compassion she had learned to conceal as her mother winced. Kate had known quite well what she meant.

'No one cares any more that I was illegitimate. *I* certainly don't,' Sophy had told her, leaning forward and hugging her warmly. 'You're the best mother anyone could ever want. You and Gran and Gramps gave me a far more secure world than most kids get, you know. I don't care that I don't have a father... that you weren't married.'

Maybe not, but Kate did... she always had, and part of her always would, Kate reflected sadly as she poured her friend's coffee now.

'Everything's well under control with the buffet,' Lucy told her, suddenly practical. 'I've got the girls organised, so they'll be here first thing tomorrow morning, and I've also told them that you aren't to so much as lift a finger,' she added severely.

'Tomorrow *you* are going to concentrate on being the most beautiful, stunning mother of the bride there ever was, and *not* on being a partner in "Removable Feasts".' The name of their catering company was a play on the common phrase 'movable feast' that had occurred to them in a flash of inspiration.

Mother of the bride... There was a huge lump in her throat, an aching tight pain in her chest... a loneliness that never really went away, as something deep inside her cried, but what about the *father* of the bride? What about the *father* Sophy had never had and should have had?

'I've called at the Fleece and checked up on the rooms. Mrs Graves is looking forward to the influx, I suspect.' Lucy looked appreciatively out of the window at the summer perfection of the lawns and flowerbeds which had been Kate's parents' pride and joy.

Kate's parents' unexpected death in the plane crash had left her bereft emotionally, but secure financially, just so long as she was careful.

With the money coming in from 'Removable Feasts' both Sophy and Lucy had urged her to give herself a few treats—to take a holiday, or splash out on new clothes—but Kate had ignored their advice. Jeans and T-shirts were her normal wear in summer, and jeans and sweaters in winter; she did not live the kind of life that called for expensive fashionable clothes, and as for a holiday... She was happiest here in her natural habitat, where she blended into its protective camouflage. She had no desire to seek out other surroundings, surroundings against which she might stand out as being different, drawing attention to herself.

Sophy often bemoaned the fact that she had not inherited her mother's silver-fair hair and perfect oval features, but to Kate her daughter, who had inherited from her father his raven-black hair and distinctive bone-structure softened into femininity, had a vigour and appeal that was far more powerful than her own pale delicacy.

Sophy had even inherited her father's height, at five feet nine standing inches above her tiny mother, who was barely five feet two; those who witnessed the daughter's protective attitude towards the mother almost always reflected rather enviously on the rapport that existed between them, despite their physical dissimilarities.

Only Kate knew how very painful she had found it at first to look at her tiny daughter and see mirrored in her infant features the features of the man she had loved and who had deserted her.

It made no difference telling herself that she had asked for what happened...that she had been a complete fool and that she deserved what had happened to her. Sophy had not deserved it, and neither had her parents, who had stood by her so wonderfully and caringly, cherishing both her and Sophy, helping her, counselling her...supporting both emotionally and financially.

Right from the start she had been determined about two things. One was that she was going to have her child, and the second was that she was never, ever going to try and seek out its father...not after she had learned the truth about him.

'Hey, come back, daydreamer,' Lucy admonished, grinning at her.

'Sorry, I missed that,' Kate apologised, flushing a little. This was no time to be thinking about the past. In another couple of hours Sophy would be here, and she wanted to devote these last precious hours with her to Sophy alone.

She liked John very much and had no doubts at all that he would make Sophy a good husband, but their lives and careers lay in London where they both had high-powered and demanding jobs, and from now on those visits that Sophy did manage to make home would of necessity include John.

'Well...soon it will all be over,' Lucy told her cheerfully. 'The culmination of six months' hard work. I've still got this to go through,' she added ruefully. 'And with Louise only sixteen and Joe ten, it's going to be a good few years before I have to start planning weddings. What time's the florist arriving?'

'Some time this afternoon,' Kate told her. She glanced up at the kitchen clock. 'Which reminds me, I've got to go and collect the strawberries. I'd better get a move on.'

'I'll be over later this afternoon with the salmon and the rest of the stuff,' Lucy promised, finishing her coffee and giving a wry sigh. 'How on earth do you manage to stay so calm and organised? If I were you, I'd be falling to pieces...'

Kate smiled at her, but said nothing. She could have told her friend that having gone through the crucible of fire into its heart, long, long ago, there were now very few situations which could test her

self-control to its limits. She had learned long ago
to conceal her feelings...to protect herself and
others, and it had been a deeply painful lesson.

The morning flew by. Despite all her careful arrangements there were still small hitches...things
to be done. She was running half an hour late by
the time she collected the strawberries. On the way
back, driving the hatchback estate car which she
had had specially fitted with stable trays for carrying food, she slipped a favourite Bruce
Springsteen tape into the machine, trying to relax
as the familiar voice and music filled the inside of
the car.

She was just turning into her own drive, when
he started to sing 'If you're looking for love', and
her heart somersaulted with idiotic pain, her mouth
compressing as she reminded herself that at thirty-
seven she should be long past the stage of being
affected by a pop song. And it wasn't even as
though she *were* looking for love. After Sophy's
birth, she had determinedly and resolutely turned
her back on the idea of love and marriage.

When her mother had tried to talk to her gently
about her attitude, she had said bitterly that she
could never expect anyone else to take on both her
and her baby, declaring flatly that she was second-
hand and used. Her mother had protested vigor-
ously at her claim, telling her gently that she had
nothing to feel ashamed about, and that no man
who loved her would ever blame her for what had
happened...that men these days did not expect their
wives to come to them without having had any pre-

vious sexual experience. But she had shaken her head and said it was not the lack of her virginity she had meant, but the loss and destruction of her self-worth and trust...the fact that she would never be able to give to anyone else all that she had given so trustingly and eagerly to Joss...and that it was because of that that she, and her emotions, would be second-hand.

She had stuck resolutely to her decision and, over the years, as her first initial terrible shock and grief had softened, she had wondered if perhaps her life was not after all more surrounded by love, more filled with contentment than many a woman's who did have a husband and a father for her children. She thought of that woman who was so closely linked to her and yet who knew nothing of her existence, and wondered what *her* life had been. What must it be like to be married to a man who cheated...who lied and deceived. How very much more destructive that must be...a festering, poisonous wound as opposed to the clean, almost killing one she had received—and *survived*!

She stopped the car and got out, and as she did so the kitchen door opened and she saw Sophy standing there, grinning at her.

Her heart flooded with love and pleasure. She ran towards her and they hugged one another.

'Hello, little mama,' Sophy whispered tremulously, reverting to the silly pet name which had evolved when she was tiny and people had confused Kate's role in her life. She had then started calling Kate 'my little mama' and the nickname had stuck, especially when Sophy had started shooting up above her mother.

Once she had released her, Kate stepped back to look at her daughter. This incredibly special and beautiful child who she still could not entirely believe was hers.

Every bit of her gleamed with vitality and happiness, right from the crown of her silky bobbed hair to the polished nails of her toes, peeping through the high-heeled sandals she was wearing.

Looking at them, Kate remarked absently, 'It's just as well John is so tall.'

'Mm.' The dark grey, black-lashed eyes that Sophy had inherited from her father gave Kate a laughing look, as the girl said irrepressively, 'We fit very well together...'

She had never been able to resist teasing, and she laughed again as she saw the faint surge of colour sting her mother's face. 'Don't worry, little mama,' she added chidingly. 'I'm not about to repeat *your* mistake. I am most definitely not pregnant. At least, not yet,' she added thoughtfully.

There was a small silence, and then Kate said emotionally, 'You, my love, are most definitely the best mistake I ever made.'

It was true. Nearly twenty-one years ago, terrified, pregnant... she had just made the discovery that the man she thought loved her was in fact married to someone else... had had a child with that someone else. She had thought then that her whole world had come to an end, and so it might

have done if her parents hadn't been so
wonderful...

If... so many ifs, which had brought her to this
day and this place, surely one of the proudest
women alive.

She had achieved so much, this daughter of
hers... done so much in her short life. A first-class
degree from Oxford... holidays spent working
abroad, so that she could be self-supporting, a wide
circle of friends, leisure activities that ranged from
skiing to abseiling... A job that promised to sustain
her intellectually all through her life... and now
marriage to a man who would genuinely be a true
partner to her; moreover, a man whose family had
opened its arms to welcome her.

With fervent gratitude she acknowledged that,
whatever her own feelings about the circumstances
of Sophy's birth, her daughter had never betrayed
a moment's chagrin or resentment over them. She
was a girl who was naturally likeable, who was open
and friendly with others, who met life on its own
terms. Sophy had grown so much into being the
woman she herself had always wanted to be and
never could be, and now here she was, adult, con-
fident, in love, with the whole world spread out in
front of her for the taking.

Kate felt her heart swell with maternal pride... a
pride that was tinged with sadness. It was an in-
trinsic part of Kate's personality that she took no
credit herself for Sophy's well-adjusted attitude to
life.

Today marked the start of a new life for
Sophy... and the end of an old life for her.

'Well, come on,' Sophy demanded. 'Let me see what you're planning to wear tomorrow...I can't wait to see the guests' faces when they realise that you are my mother.'

Tears stung Kate's eyes. It was an added gift, this one—that Sophy should always have been so proud and supportive of her...almost as though from a young age she had known how vulnerable she was.

She touched her arm now and smiled through her tears.

'*You* are the one everyone will be focusing on,' she chided her maternally, and then a frown touched her forehead and she said quietly, 'Sophy, I'm sorry that your father won't be here to give you away. I...'

Sophy hugged her swiftly. 'Don't be,' she told her promptly. 'Any man who could do what he did to you is a rat and, quite honestly, I wouldn't want him in my life. I mean it,' she assured her firmly, and then added, 'John's mother was asking me the last time I saw her if I ever wondered about him, or was curious about him.'

'What did you tell her?' Kate asked her quietly. It had always hounded her, this fear that one day Sophy would naturally want to seek out the man who had fathered her. Her fear had not been for herself but for her child...that Sophy would be rejected as she had been rejected.

'The truth. That you explained to me when I was old enough to understand what had happened... That you had fallen in love with someone who you thought was free to love you in return...and that you had then discovered that he was in fact already married with a child. That on the advice and counselling of Gran and Gramps you had decided not to get in touch with him and tell him about me because, as they had pointed out to you, he had already made it plain that he didn't want anything to do with you, and that anyway, a man who had already betrayed his marriage vows and his child was only going to cause us both a great deal of unhappiness.

'I've always agreed with what Gran and Gramps told you,' she added calmly. 'He couldn't have been much of a man, to hurt you the way he did. You and Gran and Gramps have always given me so much love . . . been so honest and truthful with me.' She looked steadily at her mother. 'I admire you tremendously for not giving in to the temptation to confront him with your pregnancy, especially when you loved him so much. He has no place in my life or in my heart. How could he have? If I had one wish it would not be for my father, but that Gran and Gramps were still alive and that Gramps was here to walk down the aisle with me.'

They hugged one another silently for a moment, both of them acknowledging the huge emotional debt they owed to Kate's parents, who had always been so wise and caring, never reproaching her for what she had done but instead gently helping her to understand that for her own sake and her child's she must put the past behind her.

'I think what you and I need right now is a bottle of champagne and a weepy movie,' Sophy said shakily.

Kate laughed.

'Maybe, but what we have is a potential strawberry mountain waiting to be hulled and washed.' She saw Sophy's grimace and reminded her, mockseverely, 'You were the one who wanted the June wedding...the country setting...the fresh strawberries and cream...'

'Don't remind me,' Sophy protested as they went together to the car to bring in the fruit.

CHAPTER TWO

'THE MOST beautiful girl...'

'Such a lovely dress...'

'What a fabulous day...'

The comments washed past Kate as she stood on the steps of the church with Sophy and John and John's immediate family.

The June sunshine was dazzlingly bright and hot after the cool, cloistered peace of the church. The vicar had held a private memorial service for her parents in that same church after the plane crash... Her breath locked in her chest as she reminded herself that, today of all days, she must not allow anything to cloud Sophy's happiness.

And Sophy *was* happy. It radiated out of her.

As she watched, the newly married pair touched hands, a small, private gesture of shared love and reassurance, and then Sophy commented curiously, 'Heavens, John, who's that gorgeous dark-haired man over there with the redhead?'

All of them turned to look in the direction Sophy was discreetly indicating.

A couple were standing apart from the rest of the guests, in the shadowy seclusion of the quiet graveyard.

Kate looked at them absently, and then focused abruptly on the man, her heart feeling as though it had suddenly been clamped in a giant vice. The whole world seemed to spin crazily around her as her throat went dry, and she fought off the panic engulfing her. It couldn't be... Not here! Not now! Not today!

Somewhere in the distance John was pretending to be jealous, and his mother was saying in amusement, 'That's my cousin, Joss Bennett.'

'Oh, is it? I've heard you mention him,' Sophy was responding, enlightened. 'Funny, I'd envisaged him being much older than that.'

'You mean rather more around my age,' John's mother teased.

Kate heard their conversation. It lapped round her, a lulling, distant noise that couldn't calm her jangled, discordant nerves. She was concentrating on the man standing within the shadows of the ancient yews, sunlight dappling his features, obscuring them slightly, but not so much that she had not recognised him immediately.

It had been almost twenty-two years ... by rights her heart and mind should have forgotten everything about him ... but they hadn't.

She had a confused awareness of a desperate need to keep up appearances, to act as though nothing untoward had happened ... as though she hadn't looked across a sun-dappled churchyard and seen standing there the man who had deserted her all those years ago, leaving her to bear his child ... this child who was now a young woman.

Somewhere in the distance, John's mother was saying easily, 'Well, of course, Joss is much younger than me, I suppose now he must be forty-two, going on forty-three.'

'He doesn't look it,' Sophy was saying admiringly. 'Heavens, I would have thought he was somewhere in his late thirties at the most.'

'Hey,' John cautioned her teasingly. 'Watch it ... I'm beginning to get worried. I shall definitely *not* introduce you to him.'

The sun's heat, the laughter and warmth of the day ... all of them might not have existed, Kate felt so cold and alone.

Was it mere coincidence that had brought him here today of all days, or ... ?

It *was* coincidence! It *had* to be. If by some remote chance he had discovered that Sophy was his child, surely he wouldn't have waited until today, until she was getting married, to claim their relationship?

The vice loosened its grip a little. She drew a deep, shaky breath, trying to control the trembling she could feel threatening her composure. It was just a horrible coincidence. He was John's mother's cousin, a coincidence ...

Someone touched her arm and she turned her head to look into Sophy's concerned eyes.

'Are you all right, Mum? You've gone quite pale, and you feel cold.'

Momentarily she was the focus of the small group's attention. This was Sophy's day, she reminded herself fiercely, and nothing was going to be allowed to spoil it. Nothing. She could see that John's mother was already beginning to frown a little, as though picking up the vibrations of shock emanating from her ... the kind of shock that had nothing to do with a beloved daughter getting married.

'It was colder than I'd expected inside the church,' she managed, forcing herself to smile.

The outfit she had chosen for the wedding consisted of a black and white silk spotted dress with short cap sleeves, in a vaguely twenties style, with a plain white silk jacket and a white silk hat trimmed in black, the colours being perfectly acceptable since Sophy had chosen to wear a dress of heavy cream silk rather than the traditional white she had claimed would look awful with her olive-tinted skin.

Skin she had inherited from her father, Kate acknowledged, unable to resist darting another tormented look at the couple in the churchyard.

They were standing facing one another, Joss bending towards the redhead while she removed something from the lapel of his jacket. She was tall, almost as tall as Sophy, and he didn't have to angle his head far to look down at her. When he had been with *her* . . . Her heart jolted frantically in her chest as memories she didn't want came surging past the barriers of her self-control. Memories of the first time they had met on the cliffs beyond the windy Cornish fishing village, devoid of tourists during that wet cold summer. She had run into him, having got caught out in the rain. She had been running back to her mother's aunt's cottage, her head down, not looking where she was going.

He had caught hold of her as she staggered, and she had lifted her head to apologise and had promptly fallen fathomlessly in love, as only a girl of just sixteen could.

He had seemed so distant and sophisticated: almost twenty-two to her sixteen, a huge distance in terms of life experience. He was already a man, she still a child, but he had offered to walk back to her aunt's with her, offering her a few personal details about himself as he did so. It was over a mile from the clifftop path to the village where her great-aunt lived, and despite the buffeting wind and icy rain she had wished it might be twenty.

When he had told her how old he was, she had lied about her own age, claiming to be nineteen.

He had almost caught her out, asking her what she was doing, what kind of post-school training, but she had fibbed that she was having to resit A levels and so was having an extra year at school.

She hadn't known then what had made her lie about her age, only that she desperately wanted to be seen as his equal and not as a silly adolescent schoolgirl.

She had been speechless with bliss when he'd asked her out. He'd been working in Cornwall for the summer, a job with the National Trust, helping to maintain the cliff-paths. He'd been lodging in the village at a house not far from her aunt's...and so it had begun.

'Mama...the photographer's ready.'

Sophy's calm, firm voice broke into her private world. She blinked, and the vision of the tall, dark-haired young man who had charmed and delighted her so much was gone, and in its place she saw the reality of a man in his forties who, as Sophy had so rightly said, could easily have been mistaken for someone in his late thirties—a man who wore his obvious wealth and sophistication as casually as the boy she had known had worn his jeans.

The arrival of the photographer gave her a much-needed excuse to slip into the background and be alone. The shock of seeing Joss so completely unexpectedly had made her feel sick and faint. Long, long ago she had accepted that he was gone from her life and that it was right that he should have done so, so that to see him here today of all days was appallingly painful. The redhead must be his wife...and she, like Joss, looked younger than her forty-odd years. She gave another quick, hunted look at the woman's immaculate make-up and hair. Her clothes were expensive, designer label most likely, but there was a petulant set to her mouth and a frown marring her forehead. Where was their child? Odd that she had never known whether it was a boy or a girl...Sophy's half-brother or -sister. Her heart gave a frantic twist as the pain splintered inside her. Still, after all this time, when it should have long ago died.

She was starting to shake. Another moment and her distress would be so obvious that it would cause comment. There were still the photographs to get through, and then the reception. The day seemed to stretch endlessly in front of her, like some kind of refined torture.

What would happen when they met? Would he recognise her...and, if he did, would he acknowledge her...or pretend that they had never met?

The latter, most probably. And what about Sophy, standing there with John, laughing up into her bridegroom's face? She would go through the rest of her life never knowing that John's mother's cousin was in reality her own father.

Her heart seemed to bolt with fright. If only her parents were still alive... If only she had someone to turn to... to confide in.

She felt a light touch on her shoulder and jumped in panic, but it was only Sophy's godfather, James Phillips, the local doctor.

'Are you OK?' he asked her frowningly. Today he had stood in for the father Sophy had never had and the grandfather she had lost... giving her away... Tears rose and stung her throat and the backs of her eyes.

'Just being sentimental and stupid,' she assured him.

'Ma... the photographer wants you,' Sophy called, and distractedly she hurried over to join John's parents, while James followed at a more leisurely pace.

It was a nightmare. It couldn't be real... but it was, and sooner or later she was going to have to come face to face with Joss. She shuddered sickly, and the photographer frowned. It was normally the bride who looked faint and sick, and not her mother... although this particular bride's mother was rather unusual, slim as a gazelle, and young enough to pass for the bride's sister. It seemed impossible to believe the reality of their relationship. She must have been a child herself when she had had her, he reflected consideringly.

She was a very beautiful woman, and would have been more so if she had not looked quite so strained.

When the photographer had finished, Mary Broderick, who had seen three daughters married herself, went over to Kate and said quietly, 'It's awful, isn't it? You know you should be happy for them...and yet you feel so lost, and you hate yourself for feeling like that. It does get better,' she informed Kate with a smile.

Privately, when John had announced that he was getting engaged and had explained the circumstances of his new fiancée's birth, she had been worried about the situation, but she needn't have been. Sophy was everything she could have wanted in a daughter-in-law, and as for Kate...

Something about the petite woman who was now her son's mother-in-law made her want to mother her in much the same way she had mothered her own four children. It wasn't that Kate wasn't mature and capable. She was both. The way she had brought up Sophy was testimony to that. No, it was her vulnerability—that and the youthfulness of her face and figure. No one looking at her would ever have imagined she was a day over thirty.

'We'd like you to come and spend a couple of days with us when you can spare the time. We feel we've hardly had an opportunity to get to know you yet.'

There was no doubting the sincerity and warmth of the invitation, but Kate could barely respond to it. The moment she was dreading was fast arriving, and it was too late now to bitterly regret that Sophy had ever opted for the formality of a receiving line.

There was no way of avoiding it. She and Joss were going to come face to face.

Face to face with the man who twenty-one years ago had given her her dearly beloved daughter, and who had then walked out on her without even knowing that she had conceived.

The garden was everything a country garden should be, the scent of roses, from the traditional walkway bisecting the lawn, heady with musk. All around her Kate could hear people commenting appreciatively as they congregated on the drive. A light breeze stirred the blue and white awnings of the marquee.

The staff she and Lucy had hired to serve the meal were moving deftly among the guests, gently encouraging them on to the lawns as they circulated offering pre-wedding breakfast drinks.

James took her arm and gently guided her towards the marquee where it had been decided they would line up to receive the guests. Slowly the guests filed past, all of them beaming their pleasure and enjoyment of the day. Old friends, whose faces were as familiar to her as her own ... strangers, people who belonged to John's side of the family, but who nevertheless were reaching out to her with warmth; all of them passed her in a blur, until the shocking moment she had been waiting for, and she heard John's mother exclaiming warmly, 'Joss! It's lovely to see you. We weren't sure you could make it ...'

And then she heard the familiar timbre of a voice she had never, ever forgotten. A voice that had whispered such things to her that she had shivered in unbearable pleasure and arousal, now saying mundanely, 'We only just made it, but it's lovely to be here.'

Sophy was speaking to him, flirting lightly with him, and then it was John's turn ... John who was turning to introduce her to him.

'You won't believe it, but Kate is my new mother-in-law,' he said gallantly, and the whole world stood still as they looked at one another, and she saw from his face that this meeting was as much a shock to him as it was to her.

'Kate,' he said hoarsely, and the hand touching hers gripped her so tightly that she actually winced with pain.

He had aged, but only slightly. He was no longer a young boy, but a man ... tall, dark, powerful, his jaw lean and clean-cut, bearing no trace of too self-indulgent living, his skin bronzed and his grey eyes as clear as those of his daughter.

His hair was just as thick and dark as she remembered, and his body as he had walked towards her had moved lithely and easily.

He was a man in his sexual prime, she recognised numbly, and it didn't need the sidelong looks the other female guests were giving him to tell her so.

Shock absorbed her and held her, and then abruptly released her so that she started to shake and her eyes stung with tears. Totally unable to hold on to her composure, she tugged her hand from his and looked past him to the woman accompanying him. *Her* mouth had tightened into an unattractively thin, tight line. She glared pointedly at Kate

as she stretched out her hand, and Kate said mind-
lessly, 'Mrs Bennett.'

John waited until they had gone past to chuckle
and say to her, 'Not Mrs Bennett as yet, although
I suspect she's hoping to be. She's Joss's secretary.'

His secretary. A cold, sour sickness rose up inside
her. So he hadn't changed, she thought bitterly. He
was still the same lying cheat who had deceived *her*.
And yet outwardly he looked too uncompromis-
ingly honest and steadfast...

His appearance was as deceitful as his nature.
Where were his wife...and his child? Something
inside her twisted painfully as she stopped concentrating on the line-up of guests waiting to smile and
shake her hand, and remembered instead the
shocking agony of that cold, blustery September
day when, not having heard from Joss for almost
twenty-four hours, she had gone round to his
lodgings to find out why he had broken their date.
She had discovered from his landlady that he had
packed his bags and gone... 'Gone back to his wife
and child,' she had told her maliciously, leaving
only the cursory message that their affair was over
and that she was not to try to get in touch with him.

She could remember even now the pebble-hard
acidness of the woman's cold eyes...and how, despite her casual attitude, she had sounded as though
she had enjoyed delivering Joss's message.

She had only met the woman on a couple of pre-
vious occasions. Normally she and Joss met just
outside the village on the cliff-path. She hadn't liked
his landlady then, and she had liked her even less
at that moment.

Joss, married. She had hardly been able to take it in. He was still only a student, in his last year at Oxford and, although she had surmised from the odd comments he had made about them that his family had money, he had said nothing to her to indicate that his family consisted of anything more than parents, and various aunts, uncles and cousins. He had certainly never intimated that he was married...and not just married, but a father as well.

His landlady had watched her unkindly, callously smiling at the tears she had been unable to stop stinging her eyes.

'What did you expect?' she had scoffed. 'He was just using you, that's all. Did you really think he intended it to be anything more than a brief fling? He's told me not to give you his address. So don't bother asking for it,' she had added brutally and triumphantly, starting to close the door.

Numb with pain and shock, somehow or other Kate had managed to drag herself back to the cliff-path which had been their trysting place. She still could not take it in. Only forty-eight hours ago he had held her, kissed her, whispered to her that he loved and wanted her...and she had thought that implicit in those words was a promise for the future. And now...

She started to tremble violently realising what she had done. She had given herself to him with joy and fervour...given herself to a man who was already committed elsewhere...a man who was married with a child.

Mercifully, then, she hadn't known that it wasn't only a broken heart he had left her with.

She had only discovered she was pregnant six weeks after she had returned home. Shocked and bewildered, she had made no attempt to hide the truth from her parents; they, having observed the stunned, silent state in which she had returned to them after her holiday, had already guessed that some emotional trauma was at the root of her distress.

It had not occurred to them that it might be more than a mere holiday romance that was making her so pale and listless until she started being so violently ill.

After that...she had told them haltingly and miserably what she had done, how she had betrayed the mores they had taught her, how defiled and unhappy she felt, not at making love with Joss—that she could not regret—but at having made love with him believing him to be free when he wasn't...at having participated, however innocently, in the breaking of marriage vows she considered to be sacred.

Her parents had been marvellous...wonderfully supportive and caring.

She had never gone back to the village. There had been no point...her mother's aunt, disgruntled with the appalling summer weather, had sold the cottage and moved back to London, announcing that country living was not for her, and Joss had been someone she had resolutely shut away in a dark corner of her mind, refusing to allow herself to think about.

Except when Sophy was born...except when her parents died...except this morning, dressing for the wedding and grieving for all that might have been.

Seeing him had shaken her out of those idiotic daydreams, reminding her of what reality was. Reality was a man who had cold-bloodedly seduced her knowing that he was committed elsewhere, and who, it seemed, still continued to break those same marriage vows he had broken with her.

No wonder he had been so shocked to see her. He was probably wondering how quickly he could make his excuses and leave.

As the thought formed, she looked across the flower-decked marquee and saw him standing with a group of people, but slightly to one side of them, as though apart from them. He was looking directly at her, the grey eyes focusing on her with such intensity that for a moment she actually took a step towards him.

'Kate, the girls are getting twitchy about serving the buffet,' Lucy came up to warn her.

Thankfully Kate turned aside and glanced at her watch.

'Yes. We'd better get everyone sitting down.'

Sophy and John had opted for an informal arrangement of round tables in the marquee, apart from the top table for close members of the family, and as James tactfully organised the ushers into making sure that everyone found their tables and sat down Kate turned her back on Joss and escaped.

The meal was a blur of tension and misery. Conversation hummed around her, Sophy and John as euphoric as the bubbles in the champagne. Someone—one of John's married sisters, she thought vaguely—complimented her warmly on the food. She smiled, feeling as though her whole face had become frozen.

Joss was sitting right in her line of vision; the redhead clawed possessively at his arm whenever his attention wavered from her, and Kate thought viciously that he deserved the other woman's petulant possessiveness.

All through the toasts and speeches she was conscious of growing tension, of an anxiety that balled in her stomach and made it impossible to concentrate on anything bar the dark-haired man sitting just within her vision.

Afterwards, while Sophy and John circulated among their guests, she tried to escape, but she had barely reached the opening of the marquee when Joss stopped her.

Her heart lodged painfully in her throat, her pulses hammering frantic messages of fear.

'Your daughter looks very beautiful,' he told her gravely. 'John is a very lucky man.'

Stock compliments and phrases, with no nuance in them to make her muscles tense and her eyes flicker with distraught dread... nothing in his eyes to warn her that he had guessed that Sophy was *his* child... just a fine hardening of his mouth that made him suddenly look older and very bitter as he added devastatingly, 'And so is James.'

James... She looked round wildly, her heart hammering with frantic, desperate ferocity. James was standing several yards away, talking to John's mother.

'Joss, there you are. It's time we left.' The redhead drew level with them and glowered warningly at Kate. 'You know you promised we wouldn't be staying long.'

Kate winced at her lack of manners, wondering faintly if the woman realised that she was doing her a favour and that the last thing she wanted was for Joss to linger.

She gave them both a polite, controlled smile and said brightly, 'It was good of you to come. Please do excuse me,' and quickly sidestepped them both, heading for the house and security.

It was a good half-hour before she was able to accept that they had actually gone and that she was safe, but the shock of Joss's unexpected appearance had taken its toll, and it was impossible for her to relax and enjoy what was left of the day.

By the time the last of the guests were leaving she had a pounding headache, and the last thing she wanted to do was to join John's family for the celebratory meal they had organised at the Fleece.

Sophy and John had gone. They were flying to Antigua for a three-week honeymoon, and Sophy's face had been blissfully rapt as she and John left for the airport.

'Takes you back, doesn't it?' John's mother had sighed...and had then bitten her lip in embarrassment and apologised.

'Heavens, I'm sorry...that was tactless.'

'It doesn't matter,' Kate had assured her, and then, because of the pity she could see in her eyes, she had added firmly, 'And besides, the relationship I had with Sophy's father was as important to me as though we were married. It was only later when I discovered that he already had a wife and a child.'

Mary Broderick bit her bottom lip guiltily. She hadn't meant to raise unhappy memories for Sophy's mother, and, despite her initial shock at discovering that her son's mother-in-law was a woman of thirty-seven who looked barely thirty, and who had conceived her daughter outside marriage when she was only sixteen during a relationship with an already married man, once she had met Kate she had quickly realised that, however deplorable the circumstances of Sophy's conception, her mother was not to blame for them.

'Do you never see him...hear from him?' she asked awkwardly, wanting to fill the painful silence.

Kate shook her head quickly and lied, 'And nor do I want to.'

Her head was pounding with sickening intensity. All she wanted to do was to go and lie down on her bed, but instead she had the evening to go through.

When it was all over, she would sleep for a week, she promised herself tiredly as she forced a smile to her lips and tried to appear as though she was enjoying herself.

CHAPTER THREE

OF COURSE, she didn't. On Monday morning it was
back to her normal routine of preparing the very
special sandwiches that she and Lucy delivered to
offices in York, along with their special executive
lunches.

They were frantically busy, with two of their staff
off on holiday and Kate having to drive into York
in their van to make the deliveries and pick up fresh
supplies.

After that she had an appointment with a woman
who wanted them to cater for her husband's fortieth
birthday party, and then there was an evening reception in York, but thankfully Lucy was doing
that.

The week whirled by and it was Friday before
she knew it. Thankfully she had managed to give
herself Friday afternoon off. The house was desperately untidy and needed cleaning from top to
bottom, she acknowledged ruefully, and then there
was the garden... The marquee people had been
as careful as they could, but...

Acknowledging wryly that her afternoon off was
likely to prove more arduous than working, she
rushed back from York, dropped off the fresh supplies at Lucy's home and then hurried home.

All afternoon she worked at top speed, refusing
to acknowledge that part of her determination to

keep busy was rooted in her desperate need to hold
at bay the shock of seeing Joss again so unexpectedly and unwantedly.

By six o'clock she was exhausted, but she refused to allow herself to rest. There was still the
garden to do, and it was silly not to take advantage
of the long summer evening.

She hadn't bothered to stop for lunch and she
wasn't hungry now. In fact, she hadn't been hungry
all week, and had lost a dramatic amount of weight.
Lucy had noticed it and teased her about it, saying
that it was the bride who traditionally wasted away,
not her mother, and Kate had grimly let her believe
that it was the build-up to Sophy's wedding that
had caused her to drop so many pounds, rather than
admitting the truth.

At nine o'clock, her back aching and her muscles
trembling with exhaustion, she acknowledged that
it was time to give up.

Wincing as her strained muscles protested, she
went inside and straight upstairs to her bedroom.

After her parents' death, although she had
cleared out their room, she had felt unable to move
into it, and so she was still using the bedroom she
had grown up in. She and Sophy had shared a
bathroom, her parents having their own, and she
acknowledged tiredly how empty the house felt now
that she was living in it on her own.

Showered and dried, she grimaced slightly at her
unmade-up face and wildly curling hair. All she
wanted to do was to go to bed, but there were the
books waiting downstairs for her attention...if she
could just spend a couple of hours on them now...

Tiredly she went down to the comfortably shabby sitting-room at the back of the house. It overlooked the garden and had been her parents' favourite room.

Both she and Sophy had grown up in this room with its faded chintz furniture, and its worn rugs and polished parquet floor.

She got the books out and sat down at the desk that had belonged to her mother.

She was so tired that it was virtually impossible to concentrate on what she was doing. The french windows were open, admitting the cool evening air and the musky scent of the bourbon roses.

Her back ached appallingly. If she could just lean back in the chair and close her eyes for a couple of minutes...

When the expensive Jaguar saloon car purred up over the gravel, she was too deeply asleep to hear it.

It stopped alongside her own car, the driver's door opening and then closing again with a quiet click.

The man who emerged from the car straightened up and looked warily at the silent house.

It had been a long drive from London, and an even longer week, with this meeting on his mind throughout the length of it. He had been hard pressed to leave the office early, but eventually he had managed it. The ailing company he had taken over from his father twenty-odd years ago was now high-powered and very successful, but there were times when that success tasted like ashes in his mouth.

He walked to the back door and knocked briefly on it. There was no bell, and when no one answered his summons he turned to glance back at the car parked next to his own and his frown deepened.

Her car was here, but that didn't necessarily mean that she was in. Then the faint movement of the open french windows on the other side of the back door caught his eye and he walked curiously towards them.

The light was just beginning to fade, the room illuminated by a lamp on the desk several feet away.

There were papers scattered on it; the breeze had lifted some of them on to the floor; a familiar blonde head lay on the desk, pillowed on two slender, tanned arms.

The breath locked in his throat as he stared at her ringless left hand. He took a step towards her and then another, stopping abruptly when he saw the silver photograph frame on the desk.

He focused hungrily on the photograph inside it. Her daughter. *His* daughter. Then with a bitter frown he overcame his qualms and reached out to shake her awake.

The sensation of a hand on her shoulder was at once both familiar and alien, bringing her instantly out of her exhausted doze and into alert tenseness.

As she opened her eyes she struggled to sit up, wincing as her stiff neck muscles protested.

Someone was leaning towards her, blocking out the light from the lamp so that his features were indistinct, and then he said her name and a wild shudder convulsed her.

'Kate, wake up,' he demanded peremptorily, and to her own astonishment she heard herself saying grumpily and mundanely, as though the sight of him here in her sitting-room was nothing unexpected at all.

'I am awake. What do you want? What are you *doing* here, Joss?'

Her mind, fogged by exhaustion and shock, relaxed its normally vigilant hold on her defences. She lifted her head, rubbing her stiff neck muscles and glaring at him fiercely.

'How did you get in?'

She saw the open french windows and grimaced wryly. It was her fault. She had left the french windows open.

A little to her surprise, she saw his mouth thin angrily as he too looked at the open doors.

'Anyone could have walked in here,' he told her tersely.

Her eyes widened a little as she caught the note of reproval in his voice.

'Anyone could,' she agreed drily. 'But *you* did. Why? What are you doing here, Joss?'

Her brief surge of shock-born defiance left her as he responded derisively, 'I think you already know the answer to that question. I've come to talk to you about your daughter... *our* daughter...'

He stressed the possessive pronoun, watching her with eyes that seemed to see right inside her soul. Hard, bitter eyes, that seemed to blame and accuse;

but who was he to accuse her? Why should *he* feel bitter?

He had caught her off guard, and as she struggled to reassemble her defences she licked her over-dry lips, tension seeping into her muscles and paralysing them.

'What do you mean?' she challenged, knowing as she spoke that she had hesitated for far too long.

He gave her a derisive look.

'You know exactly what I mean, Kate.'

She moved restlessly in her chair. It was hard and uncomfortable, making her feel even more physically vulnerable. She longed for the soft comfort of one of the easy chairs by the fire where she could at least relax her compressed muscles, but he was standing right in front of her, making it impossible for her to move without brushing past him.

'That was some shock, seeing you so unexpectedly like that last week—and then to discover, almost by accident, that——' He broke off abruptly. 'My cousin, John's mother, invited me to have dinner with them last Sunday. We had a most illuminating conversation.'

The grey eyes bored into her, making her heart pound with fear. She wanted to drag her gaze away, to break the hypnotic concentration of his eyes and the anger she could sense he was only just able to control.

'Sophy is *my* child.' He said it flatly, refusing to allow her the opportunity to deny it.

She moistened her dry lips again, wanting to tell him that he was wrong, but her throat muscles refused to respond to her need and she could only stare wildly and betrayingly at him, while the colour came and went under her skin.

Her exhausted brain couldn't cope with the hostility emanating from him. Last weekend she had dreaded this very confrontation...dreaded the denouement which would have ruined Sophy's wedding day, and when it had not come she had reassured herself that acknowledging Sophy as his child was the very last thing Joss was likely to do.

Safe and reassured, she had started to let go of her fear, and in doing so had rendered herself vulnerable.

Her whole body ached with shock and fear.

'I can't see the point in dragging up the past now,' she challenged him bitterly.

He stared at her for a moment as though he had never seen her before, his eyes merciless, his mouth a hard line of contempt. She focused on it despairingly and then, whether because of her fear or her exhaustion, she did not know which, she suffered the shockingly hallucinatory sensation of suddenly slipping back in time, so that when she looked at his mouth she remembered how it had felt moving against her own...how *she* had felt...almost sick with excitement and desire, wanting him so much...loving him so much...

'The point is that I have already missed out on the first twenty years of my daughter's life,' Joss told her gratingly, destroying the fragile spell of the past and jolting her into the present, 'and I do *not* intend to miss out on the next twenty. You had no right to do what you did, Kate,' he told her savagely. 'All right, so you discovered that you no longer wanted me . . . that there was no place for me in your life, but . . . What's wrong?' he asked her roughly, seeing the way the colour drained from her face, leaving it pinched and white with shock, her eyes enormous in its delicacy, their soft depths betraying her disbelief and pain.

It was a look that no one could have manufactured, painful and haunting enough to make him stop in his tracks to focus on her and study her.

'What's wrong, Kate?' he repeated less savagely.

She had started to tremble violently, her reaction so intense that he reacted instinctively to it, reaching out to clasp her wrists firmly in warm fingers as though in comfort, while he registered the frantic race of her pulse.

She made an inarticulate sound of pain in her throat and tried to stand up . . . to escape. What was he trying to do to her? Why was he trying to pretend, to lie, to hurt her more than she had already been hurt?

Her cramped muscles refused to respond to her need to get away from him, and as she tried to pull herself free and push past him her legs simply refused to support her. She fell heavily against him, with an impotent cry of frustrated panic.

The too familiar scent of him was all around her, and as she struggled to escape from it she felt his arms locking round her. The silk shirt he was wearing felt nothing like the T-shirts and rough woollen shirts he had worn before, but the body beneath it was the same, hard and warm, its scent and shape dangerously evocative of the past. The harder Kate tried to escape from the miasma of

emotions pouring through her, the more impossible escape became. Confused, exhausted, unable
to understand why he was accusing *her* of leaving
him, she felt him say her name tautly, and then,
when she made no response, swing her up into his
arms and carry her over to the chairs by the fire.
He placed her in one of them, and then stood over
her, asking tersely, 'Have you any brandy in the
house?'

She shook her head, closing her eyes. 'I don't
want any.'

'No, what you want is a damned good meal,' he
told her raggedly. 'Honestly, Kate, there's nothing
of you.'

That got through to her. She stiffened in the chair
and glared at him.

'I might not measure up to the Junoesque pro-
portions of your secretary, Joss, but that doesn't
mean that there's anything wrong with me.'

'I wasn't trying to imply that there was,' he told
her drily. 'Kate, you're suffering from shock
and——'

'Yes, I am,' she agreed fiercely, interrupting him,
'and is it any wonder? You come here trying to
claim *my* daughter,' she emphasised the 'my' and
saw him wince as though the assertion hurt him in
some way. 'You start telling me some idiotic lies
about *me* not wanting *you*, when we both know
that it was the other way round. *You* were the one
who left without a word, without anything other
than that message your landlady gave me . . .'

He had been frowning, but now suddenly he was
tensely alert.

'What message?' he rapped out sharply.

Kate stared at him, and then her mouth curled in soft bitterness.

'Can't you *even* remember what you said?' she asked wryly. 'Well, I can, Joss.' In a low, pained voice, she added almost under her breath, 'Sometimes I think every word is engraved in blood on my heart.'

She wasn't looking at him, so she didn't see the way his face changed colour, the bones beneath the skin suddenly sharp and angular.

'What message?' he repeated grimly.

She focused briefly on him, and then looked away again, repeating emotionlessly from memory.

'"Tell her that it's over... and that there's no point in her trying to get in touch with me. I don't want to see her again..." She also told me about your wife and child,' Kate added in an anguished voice looking into the hearth. It was empty now. In winter a warm fire burned in it, and she shivered, suddenly feeling cold. The central heating was off, and although it had been a warm day her skin was suddenly all goose-flesh and she was shivering.

'That's not possible.' Joss sat down abruptly, and Kate, who had caught the fierce note of pain in his voice, looked across at him.

All at once he looked gaunt... no longer the young man she remembered, but an adult male with life's experiences written on his face, his eyes shadowed with bitterness and pain.

'I'm not lying to you, Joss,' she told him quietly. 'I loved you. I believed you loved me. I had no idea that you were married——'

'I wasn't,' he told her roughly, stunning her into shocked immobility. He shook his head slowly as though he was trying to clear his thoughts. 'I need to think this through. I was called home urgently because my father was ill. He'd had a heart attack. It was in the middle of the night. I'd no way of telling you ... I left you a note, giving you my address and telephone number, begging you to get in touch with me as soon as you could. It was the only thing I *could* do. I had no idea of your aunt's surname, you'd never mentioned it, and my landlady didn't know it either. I knew you lived in the Yorkshire Dales, but we'd never really discussed our respective backgrounds in any depth. When you didn't get in touch with me, I phoned my ex-landlady. She said you'd told her that you didn't intend getting in touch...that it had just been a holiday fling...'

Kate stared at him. There was no mistaking the sincerity in his voice.

'She lied to both of us!' she said shocked. 'But *why* ... *why* would she do a thing like that?'

To her amazement she saw a dull surge of colour crawl up under his skin.

'I think I may know the answer,' he told her grimly, not looking at her. 'Grace regularly boarded students working for the National Trust, as I was, and I soon discovered that she'd got a bit of a reputation for offering more than mere board and lodging. It was understandable in a way, I suppose. She was a divorced woman in her early thirties, and I don't suppose the village offered her much in the way of male company.

'The first time she came on to me I was a bit taken aback. I'd heard about her reputation but I hadn't really believed it—and then when she appeared in my bedroom one night in the early hours...' He shrugged. 'Well, let's just say it was apparent that she was making herself available. In those days I'm afraid I was inclined to be a lot more gauche than I hope I am now. I'd just met you...and perhaps I wasn't as tactful about refusing her as I might have been.'

Kate stared at him, mature enough now to read into his remarks all that he wasn't saying.

'And you think she might have deliberately lied to both of us out of revenge?' she asked him quietly.

He shrugged tiredly. 'At least it's an explanation. We'll probably never know the truth, but I promise you I did leave that letter for you...'

She knew he was speaking the truth.

'And I wasn't married.'

'Your father,' Kate asked distractedly, not daring to allow herself to think about what he was saying. 'Did he...?'

'He died,' he told her emotionlessly. 'And I was virtually thrown into taking charge of the company. It was months before I was able to take enough time to go down to Cornwall to try to trace you. My ex-landlady swore she knew nothing about you, and by the time I made it back to the village your aunt had sold her cottage and moved.'

'Yes. She went back to London. The bad summer had convinced her that country living wasn't for her,' Kate sighed.

'You knew my name,' Joss told her quietly. 'Why didn't you register it on Sophy's birth certificate?'

He had seen that!

She looked at him and said tiredly, 'I thought you were a married man, who already owed responsibility to one child. We...that is, my parents and I had decided that although one day Sophy would have to know the truth about her birth, it would be unfair to your wife and child to risk destroying their...their peace of mind by claiming paternity...'

'And in all these years, Sophy has never once asked for my name so that she could find me?'

There was so much pain in his voice that Kate felt the colour rise in her face, as though she was in some way guilty.

'No,' she said shortly, avoiding looking at him. 'She felt, as we...that is, my parents and I, felt...that she didn't want...'

'Anything to do with me,' he finished bitterly for her.

'I had to protect her,' Kate defended herself. 'You had already rejected me...broken your marriage vows and...'

'What marriage vows?' he derided savagely. 'I *loved* you, Kate...'

The words hung on the stifling air of the small room, causing an aching, yearning sensation to twist through her. She stifled it ruthlessly. She was not sixteen any more. That knowledge steadied her.

'And I loved you,' she responded calmly, 'but at barely sixteen...'

'Sixteen?' She froze as he interrupted her sharply. 'You told me you were nineteen... You were sixteen! Oh, dear heaven! You were a child—a baby...'

There was such a wealth of self-disgust and horror in his voice that Kate reacted instinctively and compassionately, saying quickly, 'You didn't know. *That* wasn't your fault. I might have been young, Joss, but I wasn't a child. I was woman enough to conceive *your* child,' she pointed out drily, unaware of the undercurrent of triumph that softened her voice and made him look at her sharply.

'So you admit that she *is* my child,' he said tiredly. 'I just couldn't believe it when, under the influence of a few glasses of wine at dinner, Mary started to tell me about how you'd conceived Sophy and then been left high and dry by some rat of a man who was already married.' His mouth twisted. 'I didn't realise *then* that you'd actually believed that I *was* married. I thought you'd simply invented that fiction to cover your own rejection of me.' He looked remorsefully at her and said bleakly, 'You must have gone through hell...'

She had, but not in the way he thought. Her hell had been caused by the fact that she loved him, not by having his child.

'Not really,' she denied quietly. 'My parents were marvellous after they got over the initial shock. They supported me all through the pregnancy and loved Sophy to death.'

She saw the shadow darkening his eyes and offered tentatively, 'She had a very happy childhood, Joss... surrounded by love. In fact, when I felt really low, I used to try to cheer myself up by comparing Sophy's lot with your other child's, reminding myself that although Sophy might not have a father, she did have the love of three adults who cherished and adored her, while your legitimate child had a father who didn't care enough for it or for its mother to stay faithful to her...'

His face was dark with emotions that threatened the barrier of his self-control as he said tersely, 'No wonder she's never tried to get in touch with me. She must really hate my guts.' He moved his head slightly, swallowing past the rigid muscles of his throat, and Kate's heart leapt sharply as she caught the faint glitter of tears between his dark lashes.

When he bowed his head defensively, she moved instinctively, reaching out to touch the downbent dark head so like their daughter's, her touch compassionate and tender until she realised what she was doing and who he was, and snatched back her hand as though the crisp darkness of the hair beneath her fingers had actually scorched her.

'I'm sorry,' he said heavily, apparently oblivious to her brief, betraying gesture. 'It's just that it's all been such a shock... All week I've been thinking about this meeting, imagining what I was going to say to you, but the reality is so different from what I'd imagined.'

'Yes,' Kate agreed bleakly.

'Look,' he said heavily, 'I think we both need time to come to terms with what we've learned tonight. I'm staying in the village. I'll go back there now. Can I call and see you again tomorrow? There are things we need to discuss.'

What things? she wanted to ask, but in her heart she knew...and had known from the moment she opened her eyes and heard him say that possessive 'our daughter'.

It wasn't she who had brought him up here. It was Sophy. Sophy—who would have to be told that she had lied to her about Joss not wanting her. Not deliberately, it was true, but she had lied none the less, and in doing so had denied her daughter a loving relationship with her father.

She was quite sure that Joss had no intention of withdrawing from Sophy's life now. Why should he? But what would Sophy think of *her* once she knew the truth? Would she hate her, resent her...turn away from her?

Joss got up tiredly and headed for the door. She followed him automatically, and then stopped abruptly as a thought struck her.

'Joss.' He turned to look at her, his face shadowed in the darkness of the room.

'Your wife...' she said uncertainly. All right, so he hadn't been married when they met, but he most certainly must be now! 'Does she know about...about Sophy?'

He was silent for a moment and then he said tiredly, 'I don't have a wife, Kate. I was married, briefly, but we separated after less than twelve months. We're divorced now. She didn't want a family and I did. Ironic, isn't it?'

He opened the door and walked through it. She followed him, unlocking the back door for him and watching him.

He hesitated on the step for a moment, and then said softly, 'I'm sorry if tonight...upset you!'

Upset her? Tension tingled down her spine.

'It shocked me,' she admitted. 'And saddened me, of course...but what happened between us is all in the past now, and if I was upset it was because of the way Sophy has been cheated of her father...not for any personal reasons.'

Her chin tilted as she stared at him, defying him to contradict her, to claim that she still loved him. And it wasn't until he had driven off into the darkness that she asked herself just why it had been so important to her that she make it plain that she no longer felt anything for him, when he had never once implied that the existence of her long-ago love mattered to him one way or the other.

It was Sophy who had brought him to her door. Sophy who was important to him. Not her.

Of course, it was impossible for her to sleep. She lay there in bed, reliving every word he had said, trying to come to terms with the enormity of the wrong that had been done to them by a jealous, bitter woman and wondering why she did not feel more pain, more anger...wondering why she could not feel anything other than a cold, aching fear that somehow he would come between her and Sophy.

She didn't want to see him tomorrow. She didn't want to see *anyone*. She wanted to hide herself protectively away. She wanted to escape from the dreadful nightmare her life had suddenly become.

So why then, when she did eventually fall asleep, did she dream so vividly about him...about the

sensation of his mouth moving against her
own...about the sensation of his hands against her
skin, holding her, loving her with the old haunting
tenderness? She woke up aching with need, her face
damp with tears as her dreams had turned the key
in the lock she had refused to open, and once again
she had been that sixteen-year-old who had given
herself so eagerly and completely, who had given
herself with love and been given love in return.

Now, when it was over twenty years too late, she
allowed herself to recognise that there could have
been no way he could have manufactured his re-
sponses to her...his need for her...his tender, loving
initiation of her, once she had whispered to him
that he would be the first...

She moved uncomfortably in her bed. Not just
the first, but the only. Her composure suddenly
broke apart under the strain of all that had happened and she turned her face into her pillow, crying
as though she was once again that heartbroken,
devastated girl, and not a woman of thirty-seven
with a grown-up daughter of her own, and a life-
style which she had deliberately chosen to exclude
the male sex.

CHAPTER FOUR

KATE tensed as she heard a car pull into the drive and over the gravel. It was almost ten o'clock, and despite the fact that physically she was exhausted she had been unable to sleep any later than half-past six. And what sleep she had managed had not really been restorative. Her dreams had been too haunted by images from the past, by feelings and sensations she had thought long ago dead and buried.

The cumulative effect of the shocks of Joss's unexpected reappearance in her life and the discovery that he had not, after all, cold-bloodedly deceived her had had an undermining effect on her self-control.

It was ridiculous to feel like this, she derided herself, as jumpy and apprehensive as a teenager, both dreading and longing for her first date. And anyway Joss was not coming to see *her* ... he was coming to talk about Sophy.

She tensed as she heard male footsteps on the gravel, and then relaxed as she saw James's familiar silver-grey head come into view.

It was just as well that she and Lucy had arranged that she would have the weekend off, she reflected tiredly as she went to let him in. She didn't know how she would have coped with Joss's appearance if she had been committed to organising catering for a major event as well.

'I was just driving past and I thought I'd call in and see if you'd heard anything from the newlyweds yet,' James told her as she invited him into the kitchen.

'Sophy telephoned earlier in the week to let me know they'd arrived safely and that they were enjoying themselves,' Kate told him, offering him a cup of coffee.

He shook his head. 'No time, I'm afraid. You're pushing yourself too hard, Kate,' he warned her, looking directly at her. 'Try to slow down. You're not...'

'Getting any younger,' she supplied drily for him, wondering why all at once that knowledge should hurt her.

'That *wasn't* what I was about to say,' he reproved her. 'What I was going to say was that you aren't physically overstrong anyway. You're losing too much weight,' he told her bluntly. 'What's wrong?'

She gnawed on her bottom lip, wishing she could tell him the truth, but feeling that it was unfair to burden him with her problems. She was old enough to be able to deal with them herself, or at least she ought to be.

'Post-wedding blues, I suppose,' she fibbed, avoiding looking at him, her heart suddenly somersaulting as she heard another car pull up in the drive.

A confusing mixture of sensations flooded her. She wanted to turn and run and hide, and yet at

the same time her pulses were leaping in anticipation. Her breath locked in her throat, and a soft
blush of colour touched her skin, her fingers
clenching on the worktop as she stared wordlessly
towards the window.

Only when Joss actually stepped into view did
she acknowledge that a part of her had feared that
he might change his mind and simply go back to
wherever he had come from.

Feared? She examined her choice of verb
uneasily, while behind her James studied her reactions with frowning concern.

She went to let Joss in, and saw him check as he
looked across the room at James.

She introduced them, suddenly feeling ill at ease
and uncomfortable—aware of a tension leaping between them, but not knowing what had caused it,
and guessing that James must be wondering who
Joss was and why he was visiting her.

'James was just about to leave,' she said awkwardly, trying to fill the thick silence.

She saw James's eyebrows lift a little.

'So I was,' he agreed, and as he walked past her
he patted her arm and said warningly, 'Try not to
forget what I said, will you, Kate?'

'What exactly *did* he say?' Joss asked her curtly
after they had both watched him walk past the
window in silence. 'That you weren't to have anything to do with me?'

Kate's jaw dropped as she turned and stared at
him, confused by the biting challenge in his voice.
Last night he had been as caught off balance by
the truth as she had herself; this morning he was

different; this morning he was once again the man of the churchyard: distant . . . faintly austere, very much in control of the situation and himself, displaying no hint of any vulnerability.

'No . . . why on earth should he say that?'

There was a moment's silence, and then Joss taunted softly, 'He's your lover, isn't he?'

Kate was staggered. 'No, he is *not*!' she said indignantly. 'He's my doctor, and Sophy's godfather.' Pink colour stained her skin as she gave vent to her anger. 'If you must know, his comment had nothing whatsoever to do with you.'

'Your doctor?' Joss repeated frowningly. 'You're not ill, are you?'

'Not ill, no,' she responded absently, still trying to come to terms with the fact that he had thought James was her lover.

'Then what?' Joss pounced, startling her into looking up at him, her expression registering her confusion. 'You said he was your doctor. He was obviously here for a reason. You say that you aren't ill . . .'

'He's also my friend,' Kate pointed out drily. 'He'd simply called round to see me, that's all.' But she knew she wasn't sounding convincing and, exasperated both by his questions and her own reaction to them, she said tartly, 'If you must know—not that it's any of your business—he thinks I'm overdoing things, losing too much weight. I told him it was simply because of the build-up to Sophy's wedding.' She grimaced wryly. 'Most women of my age seem to have a problem keeping their weight down, not building it up. I suppose I should be grateful...'

'What exactly are you trying to imply, Kate? That you're middle-aged and menopausal?' he asked acidly. 'Come off it. You're thirty-seven years old and you look closer to twenty-seven. More like Sophy's peer than her parent...' He ran his hand through his hair, ruffling its sleek darkness and suddenly looking less austere, more approachable. 'I couldn't believe it when I saw you last week. I thought at first I must be hallucinating...either that or you had a younger sister almost identical to you... Why have you never married?' he asked her abruptly.

The question caught her off guard. She had thought he was coming here to discuss Sophy, not her.

'I...I don't know,' she fibbed, and then, seeing the ironic look he gave her, added defensively, 'There aren't that many men who want to take on a woman with a child, you know.'

'No?' He came towards her, surprising her with the speed at which he moved. She was trapped between his body and the wall behind her, panic clawing through her at his proximity. When he reached out and put his palm against the side of her face, she flinched back from him. Immediately his hand was removed and he said curtly, 'Look in the mirror, Kate—or are you blind? Last week at the wedding there were at least a round dozen men eyeing you in much the same way as a dog eyes a particularly juicy bone.'

Mingled with her shock was the realisation that
when he'd touched her he had simply been going
to turn her head in the direction of the wall mirror,
and her face stung with hot colour as she realised
how ridiculous her behaviour must appear.

'Maybe,' she agreed bitingly. 'But I doubt very
much that marriage was what they had in mind. I
don't go in for cheap affairs,' she told him icily,
drawing herself up and glaring at him. 'Besides,
my private life is hardly any of your concern, is it?'
she demanded challengingly, and then surprised
herself by asking curtly, 'Have you told your...your
secretary about Sophy?'

His eyebrows drew together in a deep frown as
he stepped back from her and then studied her.

'No,' he said urbanely. 'Ought I to have done
so?'

Sensing that he was mocking her, Kate compressed her lips. '*I* don't know,' she told him coldly.
'I suppose it depends on exactly how...personal
your relationship with her is.'

The frown darkened. 'Meaning what, exactly?'

Oh, he didn't like it when she questioned *him*
about his personal life, yet he obviously thought it
was perfectly in order for him to make odious as-
sumptions about her own relationships.

'Meaning that, last week, she was pointed out to
me as the future Mrs Bennett, and naturally, in
those circumstances, I would assume that you have
discussed with her your discovery that Sophy is your
daughter.'

He looked at her coldly, so coldly that she felt
as though the temperature in the room had actually

dropped, and then he said cuttingly, 'If you're inferring that she is my mistress, then you're wrong. My relationship with her is a purely business relationship.'

The biting contempt in his eyes stung her into retaliating sharply, 'Oh—does *she* know that?'

And then, abruptly, the fight went out of her. What on earth was she doing? She was reacting like a jealous adolescent ... and why? She had no right to be in the least curious about his relationship with the redhead ... no right at all, and still less to question him about it.

'I'm sorry,' she apologised tautly, turning her back on him. 'Of course it's none of my business——'

'But, mother-like, you want to ensure that your child is not exposed to any undesirable influences,' he mocked her acidly. 'Kate, Sophy is almost twenty-one years old. She's an adult, not a child.'

Thank heaven she had her back to him. Did he really believe her comments had arisen from maternal desire to protect *Sophy*?

It seemed he did, because he went on grimly, 'I know you're her mother, but there comes a time when every parent has to cut the apron strings. You could drive her away, you know, by being too possessive. If I were you ...'

It really was too much. She swung round, her eyes brilliant with pain and anger.

'But you aren't, are you?' she threw at him, balling her fists. 'How dare you walk in here and tell me how to relate to my daughter ... give me lectures on being an over-possessive mother? For your information, I am not over-possessive, and I need no help from you...'

To her humiliation, her voice became suspended as she struggled against the tide of emotion threatening her and was swamped by it. Hot tears sprung from her eyes and rolled down her cheeks and, furious both with herself and with him, she made to dash them away with one balled fist.

'Kate... Oh, lord, I didn't mean to upset you.'

'Don't touch me,' she warned him, but it was too late. She was already in his arms, her face pillowed against his hard torso while her tears soaked his shirt.

She could feel the heat of his hands against her spine through the fine cotton of her shirt. One of them dropped to her waist, resting on the thicker fabric of her jeans as though he was about to curve her into his body in the old familiar way, and immediately she tensed, realising.

'Let me go,' she demanded shakily, pulling back from him. It was too dangerous standing so close to him like this, breathing in the warm man-scent of him, being made dizzy by a thousand sensations and memories she had forgotten ever existed. Her heart was beating far too fast, her nerve-endings so intensely aware of him that they were practically sizzling. Her pulse was beating frantically and she could feel the familiar curling sensation gripping her stomach, rendering her achingly aware of him.

He didn't release her. Instead he slid one lean hand into her hair and tugged gently on it, so that she was forced to tilt her head back and look up at him.

'Look at you,' he said softly. 'I think you must be some kind of enchantress. You look more like a little girl than a grown-up woman.'

Fear flashed through her as he lowered his head. He saw its reflection in her eyes and tensed.

'What's wrong, Kate? You're not frightened of me, are you?'

'No,' she told him truthfully. It wasn't him that she feared, but herself. 'I'm just not used to being manhandled against my will. I asked you to let me go, remember?' she said acidly.

He released her immediately, stepping back from her, apologising formally. 'I'm sorry. For a moment I forgot.'

Kate ignored the half-murmured comment.

'You wanted to talk to me about Sophy,' she reminded him. 'If you'd like to come through into the sitting-room——'

That was better. That cool distance in her voice informed him that, whatever might have linked them together in the past, whatever she might have *once* felt for him, the present was different. *She* was different.

She led him, not into the comfortable sitting-room, but into the more formal drawing-room which she and Sophy rarely used, indicating a large armchair to one side of the fire.

He subsided into it, looking far more at ease in the formal room in his elegant dark grey business suit than she did in her jeans and shirt.

She hadn't bothered doing anything more than pull a brush through her curls when she'd got up, and dab on her customary eyegloss and lipstick,

determined not to make any special effort on his
behalf. No doubt now the lipstick and the eyegloss
were all gone and her eyes were looking as pink and
screwed up as a rabbit's, she thought wryly, her
mouth relaxing into a half-smile as she remembered the pains she had once taken to dress up for
him and impress him.

'Coffee?' she offered, silently suppressing the
memories.

He shook his head, and said tersely, 'Kate, I'd
like to ask you if you have any objection to Sophy
knowing who I am and why I haven't been around,'
he added bleakly.

It was exactly what she had been expecting, and
surely there was no real need for her heart to start
pounding like this, as though she was a threatened
animal, desperately seeking cover?

'No comment?' he said lightly when she said
nothing.

She shook her head, not yet trusting herself to
speak. When she did, her voice sounded rusty and
strained. 'What is there to say? We both know that
I can't stop you.'

'But you'd prefer me not to, is that what you're
saying? You'd prefer me to stay out of your lives?'
he pressed.

Their lives. Didn't he mean Sophy's life? She
struggled between the truth and the knowledge that
she had no right to deny Sophy the opportunity to
get to know him.

'That isn't my decision to make,' she said painfully at last. 'In the circumstances...after what
came to light last night, there is no justifiable reason

why Sophy shouldn't know the truth.' She couldn't sustain the level, thoughtful look he was giving her.

'You'll have her address, of course... John's mother...'

'Would doubtless give it to me if I asked,' he agreed curtly. 'But that isn't what I have in mind. For Pete's sake, Kate, do you really think I'd be so crass as to simply arrive unannounced; knock on her door and say, "Oh, hello, I'm your father..."—or is that what *you're* hoping I'd do?' he accused softly. His face took on a bitter, brooding look. 'I suppose it's only natural that you should feel like that... after all, looking at it from your point of view, I've hardly given you any reason to feel kindly towards me——'

'You could feel exactly the same way about me,' honesty compelled her to interrupt.

Joss shook his head. 'No, Kate. I don't blame you at all. If anything...' He sighed faintly. 'Look, I know all this has been a shock for you, but bear in mind that it's been just as much of a shock to me. To discover after all this time that...'

'That you have a daughter,' Kate supplemented for him. 'Yes, I can understand that.'

Something seemed to flicker in his eyes... some private sadness she couldn't understand.

'I was going to ask you if you could bring yourself to break the news to Sophy for me,' he said heavily, standing up. 'Selfish of me, I know, but I thought if you told her...' He gave her a brief, twisted smile. 'I don't want to shock her, you see, and——'

'You want *me* to tell her.' She got up and paced
the room in agitation, her heart pounding, and yet
wasn't what he was suggesting the best way of
breaking the news to Sophy? Wouldn't it be better
for her to hear the news from her...for her to explain to Sophy just what had happened?

'I'd have to invent some reason for visiting them,'
she said awkwardly. 'They live in London.'

'Yes, I know,' he said calmly. 'And so do I.
Perhaps a shopping trip...or a visit to friends.'

'A shopping trip!' Kate frowned doubtfully.
'Sophy's always urging me to spend some money
on myself. It would mean staying over for a
weekend. I'd have to find a hotel...'

'Leave all that to me,' Joss told her, adding
quietly, 'Does that mean that you'd be willing to
do it, Kate?'

She wanted to refuse; her own sense of self-
preservation demanded that she refuse, but when
she looked into his face what she saw there made
her swallow back her own feelings, unable to stop
herself reacting from the need she could see in him.

'Yes,' she said huskily. 'Yes, I'll do it.'

The next moment he had swept her up into his
arms, holding her so tightly that she could hardly
breathe.

'Oh, Kate...Kate...'

She heard the emotion in his voice as he buried
his face in her hair, and a huge wave of reciprocal
emotion engulfed her. In this she could empathise
with him entirely. After all, she loved their daughter
too, and she only had to put herself in his shoes to
be able to feel what he must be feeling now.

'How on earth am I going to thank you?'

She pulled away from him and said quietly, 'By making sure you never, ever do anything to hurt Sophy.'

He looked at her and said slowly, 'I shan't,' and then, while she stood motionless in front of him, he bent his head and brushed his mouth lightly against her own.

The shock of it transfixed her. Her lips parted on a shocked gasp, and just for a second the pressure of his mouth hardened and her body melted with familiar need and response, but already he had withdrawn from her, and was saying softly, 'Thank you, Kate. I'll never forget this.'

Nor would she, Kate reflected bleakly as he turned his back on her and walked over to the window.

'It's another fortnight before Sophy and John get back from Antigua,' she told him shakily, 'and then I think I ought to give them a week to settle in.'

'Yes,' she heard him agree. 'I think the best thing would probably be for me to ring you in three weeks' time and then we can make the necessary arrangements. Will you come to London by car or train?'

She hadn't thought that far ahead.

'Train, I expect,' she said puzzled. 'Why?'

'If you let me know the time it gets in, I'll make sure someone picks you up.'

She opened her mouth to tell him that wouldn't be necessary, and then closed it again.

Joss was saying something to her, but she hadn't caught it. She frowned and said, 'I'm sorry...what were you saying?'

'I was asking you if you'd care to have lunch with me,' he told her with dry irony.

The tone of his voice made her flush a little. 'Oh, that's very kind of you, but...I don't think...' she began to flounder while he watched her with cool grey eyes.

'What's wrong, Kate?' he challenged.

'Nothing,' she told him sharply. 'There's no need for you to take me out for lunch, Joss. I've already agreed to tell Sophy, and besides...besides, I've got rather a lot of work to catch up on...'

'I see.'

She couldn't understand why he was looking so angry. Surely he must be relieved by her refusal?

'What about dinner tonight, then?' he challenged. 'Or do you have another date?'

The word 'date' made her heart twist a little, bringing back as it did memories of the 'dates' they had once shared.

'No, I don't,' she retorted swiftly. 'I've already told you, I don't live that kind of life.'

She missed the sharp, speculative look he gave her, and the sadness that edged up under it.

'Well?' he prompted when she remained silent.

She swung round and stared at him. 'Well what?'

'Will you have dinner with me tonight?'

She knew she ought to refuse. There was no point in accepting, but something reckless and yearning inside her overruled her common sense.

'If you like,' she offered offhandedly.

'Such enthusiasm,' was his dry comment. 'But I suppose it's no less than I deserve. I'll pick you up at eight, shall I?'

Wearily Kate nodded, glancing at her wristwatch as she did so. It was just gone twelve; he had been here barely two hours, and in that short space of time she had run such a gamut of emotions that she felt physically and emotionally drained.

He moved and she followed him to the door.

'Until tonight,' he said quietly as he stepped outside.

Kate gave him a tight smile, already regretting her weakness.

She was regretting it even more at six o'clock when she opened her wardrobe and wondered what on earth she was going to wear. She had her pride, after all, and she could hardly appear at dinner dressed in jeans and a T-shirt, but her wardrobe was devoid of anything remotely deserving the appellation 'glamorous'... and, for some reason she was not prepared to examine too closely, glamorous was exactly what she wanted to be tonight. Then at the back of the wardrobe, she saw a long cardboard box and she frowned, pulling it towards her.

Last Christmas, when she had refused to attend Lucy's New Year's Eve party, claiming that she had nothing to wear, Lucy had arrived with this box, claiming that she now had no excuse for not attending.

In the event she had attended the party, but she had not worn the dress Lucy had bought for her.

Uncertainly she put the box down on her bed and opened it. At first glance the dress inside it was simply a plain black sliver of silk jersey with nothing particular to recommend it, but once on, as Kate had good reason to know, it was a different matter. She had been stunned at her friend's choice, wondering if it had been intended as some sort of joke, but Lucy had insisted that the dress was exactly her.

If so, it was a side of herself with which she herself was unfamiliar, Kate reflected with dry humour, picking it up and holding it in front of her.

If anything, time had dimmed her memory of the dress's shortcomings rather than exaggerated them.

It had a halter neck, and virtually no back, the fabric designed to cling to her hips and thighs, and was only spared from complete indecency by a gathered flare of diamond-pointed fabric to the front and back of the dress which acted as a kind of overskirt.

Chewing on her bottom lip, she studied it. It was glamorous all right...sexy, sophisticated...all those things that she normally avoided...the kind of dress a woman normally only wore for a man...or for another woman, when she wanted to warn her off. It was a dress more suited to Joss's red-headed secretary than to her. The thought slid into her mind like a serpent, and before she knew what she was doing she was wriggling out of her clothes and pulling it on over her head to study her reflection in her bedroom mirror.

A summer of working in the garden had given her a light tan, just enough to remove some of the dress's starkness. It was still every bit as devastating as she remembered. It still clung with overenthusiastic closeness to her skin. It still showed her a bewildering, unfamiliar image of herself, and it still made her feel acutely conscious of all that was missing from her life...which was probably why she had refused to wear it in the first place.

This was a dress for a sensual, sexual woman, not one who lived like a nun.

It was also the only dress she possessed, she reminded herself grimly. It was either that or the formal silk she had worn for Sophy's wedding, and Joss had seen that already.

Vanity, she chided herself derisively.

She took another look at herself and grimaced. It was either this or nothing, and, on balance, the dress was the better choice.

It was her own fault. She should have refused to have dinner with him when she had the opportunity. He was, after all, only being polite...only doing what he probably thought was necessary.

The trouble was, she thought, exasperated with her own inability to come to terms with her own emotional response to him, that she was reacting to him as though she was still sixteen years old, and she wasn't. They were two adults, thrown together by an uncomfortable twist of fate. The situation wasn't an easy one for either of them; Joss was obviously doing his best to treat her with cordiality and good manners, and it was down to her to respond to him in exactly the same mature, adult way.

Only her heart *would* keep somersaulting whenever she thought about him, and her body would keep on reacting to its memories of him in a way that made her pray that Joss wouldn't realise exactly what effect he was having on her.

Things were difficult enough as it was. The last complication they needed was for her to start mooning around like an adolescent in the throes of a major crush.

The trouble was that, while her brain seemed to have little difficulty in accepting the fact that she was thirty-seven years old, her body and her hormones appeared to feel differently.

Ironic that after all these years, when she had so successfully contained the mild sexual impulses which had attacked her from time to time by reminding herself of what happened when she gave in to them, she should suffer this idiotic surge of arousal the moment she saw Joss again.

She didn't need to search far for the reason. Joss had been her first and only lover; he was the father of her child, the reason she had virtually lived the life of a nun since he left her; it was not altogether unexpected that she should react so strongly to him.

Not unexpected, perhaps, but decidedly inconvenient . . . and potentially very embarrassing. Joss was no fool, had not lived a celibate life; he had been married, divorced . . . Then there was his secretary, but it had been plain to Kate that the woman wanted far more than a business relationship with him. How long would it be before he realised that the tension she exhibited when she was with him, the anxiety that filled her, the way she trembled and reacted to him were not borne of shock, but of something vastly different?

She dreaded to imagine what his reaction would be. Embarrassment ... pity ... resentment ... She went pale as it struck her that he might even suspect her of using her relationship with Sophy to get closer to him, to urge an intimacy on him that he did not want. And then she calmed down a little, reminding herself that the best way to avoid such an event was simply not to spend any time with him.

An excellent and logical decision, but she had already agreed to have dinner with him tonight, and to potentially spend more time with him in London when she broke the news to Sophy.

Come on, she derided herself as she got ready. You're a fully functioning adult with a mind of your own. You don't *need* to go into a state of collapse whenever you're with him. You've got will-power. Use it ...

Once she'd told Sophy the truth, the ball would then be in their daughter's court. If Sophy wished to further her relationship with her father, then she wasn't going to need Kate to help her to do so. She would be able to bow out of the situation. They would, after all, only be like too-long-divorced parents, each taking their part in their offspring's life, and allowing one another to live their separate lives in a civilised manner.

Civilised ... She pulled a face at herself in the mirror. All very nice, but there was nothing civilised about the way she felt about Joss.

So how *did* she feel about him?

The question stayed her. She looked blindly into the mirror, not seeing her own reflection.

That was the big question. How did she feel? After the first fierce trauma of shock had come a fierce surge of heady relief that she no longer had to hate him...that she no longer had to remind herself of what he'd done, and how, because of it, she must now even allow him into her thoughts.

She'd felt free, she recognised wryly. Free to...to what? *Love* him... What was the matter with her? They were different people from the boy and girl who had fallen in love. He had changed, and she had undoubtedly changed too. They didn't know one another. She *couldn't* love him. What she was doing was transferring her adolescent adoration of the boy on to the man, and that was crazy.

So crazy, in fact, that it was time she pulled herself together and put a stop to it.

CHAPTER FIVE

IT WAS with this admirable intention that she opened the door to Joss's knock slightly before eight o'clock.

As she heard his car, she had snatched up the lightweight black silk shawl which was all she had by way of an evening wrap to cover her bare shoulders and back, so that she was ready to accompany him out to his car as she opened the door.

As the gravel crunched beneath the unfamiliarity of her high-heeled shoes she winced a little at their sharpness on her thin soles. She so rarely wore high heels these days that she had forgotten how uncomfortable they could sometimes be, but the dress demanded them and so, gritting her teeth, she picked her way over the gravel carefully until she heard Joss say in amusement, 'I can never understand why women torture their feet with those things.'

They had reached the car, and as Kate leaned unobtrusively against it, glad of its support while she waited for him to unlock the door, she saw that instead of moving away from her and around to the driver's side he was studying the slim tanned length of her bare legs and polished toe-nails with a lazy male blatancy that made the breath catch in her throat.

How long was it since a man had looked at her like that? How long was it since she had wanted one to? Lucy and Sophy both were constantly chiding her, amused by her total lack of interest in men, complaining that she never even noticed when a man was interested in her and that she was completely oblivious to any sensual messages sent her way.

But she was far from oblivious now. Her stomach churned in tense protest and, for some reason she couldn't define, Joss's long, appreciative survey made her curl her bare toes a little in mute protest.

The silence between them seemed to grow heavy and intense until the sound of a car backfiring in the lane outside the house jolted her into an awareness of what she was doing and made her say curtly, 'I'm sorry if you don't approve, but these sandals happen to be the only thing I own that are suitable for evening wear.'

A shadow darkened his eyes as Joss stepped back from her.

'A subtle reminder of the fact that, without the financial help of Sophy's father, there hasn't been enough money to spare for such luxuries, Kate. You don't have to rub salt in the wound. I assure you I'm all too keenly aware of how very difficult things must have been for you both.'

Kate bit her lip and looked down at the drive, honesty compelling her to admit, 'Financially it wasn't really difficult . . . Mum and Dad supported us both quite comfortably, and then when they died . . . well, Dad was well insured . . .'

Her voice trailed off into silence. Joss could hardly be interested in hearing the details of her finances. As she looked upwards it came as a shock to discover that he hadn't moved.

'I'd forgotten that about you,' he said softly, puzzling her with the odd bleakness in his eyes. 'How very honest you were. Perhaps if I'd chosen to remember *that* instead of clinging on to my pride...' He stepped back from her abruptly. 'We'd better get a move on. I've booked a table at a place recommended to me by the landlady of the Fleece.'

He told her the name, and Kate reflected that it was just as well she had opted to wear the black dress. It was a newly opened and very sophisticated restaurant several miles away in a small country house which the owners were planning to develop as a very private and luxurious hotel. So far they had only got as far as opening the restaurant and, although Kate had never visited it, she had heard good reports of it.

From a business point of view, it could be an informative evening; she and Lucy did not aspire to rival the skills of the Roux brothers' trained chef who ran the restaurant, but it was always interesting to see a menu produced by a first-class expert, and there were always small hints to be picked up.

She and Lucy kept their menus simple and plain, serving the kind of food that a first class and gifted amateur cook might produce if she only had the energy and the time. They knew of more than one of their customers who had passed off their dinner-party food as her own.

She moved to one side as Joss opened the car door for her. The sleeve of his suit brushed her bare wrist, and a quiver of sensation ran through her.

She saw him frown as he registered her reaction. 'Cold?' he asked abruptly, as he waited formally for her to seat herself comfortably.

Kate shook her head, turning, averting her face so that he wouldn't see the tell-tale surge of colour washing over it. He was a good driver, skilled and patient, and in other circumstances it would have been a pleasure to sit beside him in the luxury of the powerful car, relaxing in its luxurious warmth as one of her favourite pieces of Handel flowed melodiously through the powerful speakers.

'I can switch this off if it doesn't appeal,' he offered considerately. Kate shook her head.

'No. I like it.'

She heard a soft note of warmth in his voice as he commented, 'We never really got as far as discussing our mutual taste in music, did we?'

The softness of his voice did something dangerous to her self-control.

'It wasn't really necessary, was it?' she responded sharply. 'As far as I can recall, we were too busy exploring one another's bodies to show much concern or appreciation for one another's minds.'

The acidity of her forthright statement fell a little sharply on her own ears. She knew she was simply being defensive, but she felt uncomfortably aware of a degree of truculent resentment in her voice which sounded more gauche than dismissive.

'Not quite true,' Joss corrected her. 'We *did* do a lot of talking . . . or at least I did. I'm afraid I was rather boringly selfish in those days . . . in more ways than one,' he added under his breath, causing Kate to drop her defensive manner and say impulsively to him,

'No, you weren't. I was grateful to you for telling me so much. At first I was so shy and embarrassed, I wouldn't have known what to say. You overawed me a little.'

'Did I?' He sounded almost amused. 'I didn't notice it. All I could think about was that I was with the most beautiful girl I'd ever seen and that I was fathoms deep in love. I never meant to hurt you, Kate . . .'

'No,' she agreed, and then, because she could not allow herself to fall any deeper into the dangerous trap in which she was already floundering, she said curtly, 'It's all in the past now, anyway. We're different people . . . adult. That's all behind us.'

'Is it?' Joss questioned her sharply. 'Can it ever be truly behind us when together we produced a child?'

Kate was thankful to see the turning for the restaurant looming up ahead of them, preventing her from having to reply, and she was even more thankful she had remained silent when Joss brought the car to a halt in the car park and said heavily, 'I suppose you're right. It doesn't do to dwell too much on the past.'

* * *

The meal they were served was everything Kate had imagined and more. The restaurant did not provide a choice of dishes, merely one menu which was served in the manner of a banquet.

When it was over they were told that coffee would be served in the drawing-room, and for those guests who wished to take advantage of it a small combo would be playing in the conservatory so that people could dance.

'Which is it to be?' Joss asked her easily, getting up to come over and stand by her chair. 'The drawing-room or the conservatory?'

'The drawing-room, I think,' Kate told him wryly. 'I'm rather past the age for dancing.'

Instantly his eyebrows drew together in a sharp frown.

'Kate, this is about the fifth time this evening you've made reference to your age, and I can't think why, unless it's to underline the fact of my own, and to subtly remind me that I'm now a man in my forties. *You* are thirty-seven years old; you've barely reached the age at which the French consider a woman to have come into her prime. You're not Methuselah.'

'And this isn't France,' Kate told him, flustered, as he pulled out her chair so that she could leave the table. Did he think she had been deliberately fishing for compliments by harping on about her age? All she had wanted to do was to make it clear to him that she was aware of the fact that she was a mature woman, and that he was here with her because she was the mother of his daughter, and not because he was attracted to her. All she had wanted to do was to make it clear to him that she was aware of the realities of their situation.

She swung away from him abruptly, feeling flustered and embarrassed, heading for the drawing-room, but he caught up with her half-way across the room and, taking hold of her arm, firmly guided her in the direction of the conservatory instead.

'*You* may consider yourself to be ready for the fireside and old age,' he told her smoothly. 'But *I* can still appreciate the pleasure of dancing with a beautiful woman in my arms.'

The words 'beautiful woman' jarred and she pulled away from him, her eyes blazing.

'I'm not your secretary, Joss,' she told him irately. 'There's no need to pander to my vanity by pretending you see me as a physically desirable woman.'

They were standing within a few feet of the entrance to the conservatory, and his hand on her arm stayed her.

'What makes you think that I don't?' he asked her dispassionately.

Kate's mouth thinned.

'You're taking good manners too far,' she told him crisply.

'Am I?' he said wryly, giving her an oblique look. 'Kate, if you're so convinced that at thirty-seven you are no longer seen as a desirable, sensual woman, I can only think that you must consider me at forty-two to be past all hope.'

'Don't be ridiculous,' she told him sharply. 'It's different for a man.'

'Not these days,' he returned equably. 'Look at Joan Collins...Sophia Loren, Linda Evans, to name just a few. Is it really that you consider yourself to be so old that no man could possibly find you desirable, or is it that you find such an assumption a convenient self-delusion to hide behind?'

Kate frowned at him. 'I don't know what you mean.'

'No? How many relationships have there been in your life, since you had Sophy, Kate?'

She gave a tiny, outraged gasp of anger. 'That's none of your business,' she began, only to be interrupted as he said coolly,

'No, it isn't, but that doesn't give me an answer. I think you're deliberately hiding from your own sexuality...deceiving yourself into believing that you aren't desirable. Open your eyes, Kate. You are a very beautiful woman...a very warm and compassionate woman.'

When she refused to turn her head and look at him he said fiercely, 'Have you any idea what you're doing to me? How guilty you're making me feel? *Is* it because of me that you've developed this ridiculous belief that you're undesirable...because you believe *I* rejected you? Because if so...'

Kate had endured enough.

'No, it is *not* because of you,' she lied. 'You have *no* reason at all to feel any guilt. There...satisfied?'

The evening was fast becoming a nightmare. Joss was pushing past the 'no trespassing' signs she had put up as her defence, and ruthlessly raising subjects she had no wish to discuss.

As she looked up at him and saw that he was looking cynically unconvinced, she said bitterly, 'Don't you think you're being rather arrogant, Joss? All right, so there hasn't been a succession of lovers in my life, but that has nothing to do with you ... not directly. When Sophy was a baby she took up all my time and attention, and then later ... well, I was content with my life the way it was, and I still am.'

She saw that he was looking at her oddly.

'Kate,' he interrupted her huskily, 'are you saying that there hasn't been *anyone* in your life since me?'

Too late she saw the trap. She looked wildly at him, and then away from him, longing to be able to lie, but knowing she had left it too late.

'I don't think there's any point in this discussion,' she said defensively, and then added, 'I'm tired, Joss. I'd like to go home. It's been a long day.'

'You haven't had your coffee yet,' he pointed out, and somehow or other she found herself being guided to one of the small tables tucked discreetly into the shadowy foliage that clothed the walls of the conservatory.

The combo were playing waltz music and several couples were dancing, not all of them as old as Kate would have imagined; she noticed several couples on the floor who could only have been in their mid to late twenties.

The coffee was served with delicious hand-made chocolates, but Kate had no appetite for them. For some reason Joss seemed to keep prising out of her things she would much rather have kept to herself.

She was looking broodingly into her empty coffee-cup when he said abruptly, 'Would you like to dance?' and before she could refuse he was on his feet, drawing her to hers, and propelling her unwilling footsteps in the direction of the polished dance-floor.

She and Joss had never danced together before, and in view of her tension and nervousness she fully expected to find that she was falling all over his feet and making a complete fool of herself, but instead, once he had taken her in his arms, something almost magical seemed to happen, so that within seconds she was gliding over the floor, her steps matching his as though they were made to go together.

Kate had waltzed before at a variety of social functions with a variety of partners, but never before had she experienced the dangerous intimacy which had once made the dance forbidden to un-married girls because of the dangerous manner in which it allowed a man to actually touch the bare flesh of his partner.

And Joss *was* touching her bare flesh, his hand resting firmly against the small of her back, curving her into the intimacy of his own body so that with every movement she was conscious of the maleness of him.

When she felt the hardness of his arousal pulsing against her she went rigid with shock, almost stumbling as she missed a step.

'What's wrong, Kate?' Joss whispered against her ear. 'Still not convinced that you're capable of arousing desire . . . ?'

That *she* should be embarrassed, while he appeared to be totally unfazed by his reaction to her, stunned her into silence. But the heat and pressure of him against her wasn't something she could easily distance herself from, and shatteringly, within seconds of recognising his reaction to her, her own body was responding to it. Before, when she had almost demanded that he release her, now she was praying that the music wouldn't end, and Joss would not see the shaming, humiliating evidence of what was happening to her in the swollen hardness of her nipples which were even now pushing eagerly against the thin stretch jersey of her dress, as though clamouring for his visual attention. If he stepped away from her now... She went hot at the thought, and then cold as she wondered if his apparent arousal was simply something he had manufactured by thinking of someone else, his secretary perhaps, just to prove a point to her... If so, it was even more vital that she didn't allow him to see just how much he was affecting her.

Because she dared not allow herself to leave the floor until she had got her rebellious body under control, she nodded when the tune changed and Joss asked if she wanted to stay on the floor or return to their table, but in the end it made no difference. Nothing she could do or say to her wanton flesh seemed able to stop it from flaunting its response to him, and in the end she had to suffer the appalling tension of stepping away from him and quickly turning her back on him as she headed for their table, praying that he wouldn't look properly at her until she had managed to wrap herself in the protection of her shawl.

'Cold?' he enquired solicitously, watching her do so.

She managed a brief, tight smile. 'A little . . . and tired. I'd really like to go home, Joss.'

Just for a moment it seemed as though he was going to argue, as though it might even be disappointment that was shadowing his eyes, but Kate knew she was imagining things.

'You're right,' he agreed calmly. 'I've got an early start in the morning. I'm flying to Germany on Monday on business.'

'Will your secretary be going with you?'

The moment the words were out, Kate regretted them. Colour stung her face, and she said in a stifled voice, 'I'm sorry.'

'There's no need to be,' Joss told her easily. 'She doesn't always accompany me when I go abroad, but on this occasion she will be going. Her German is more fluent than mine.'

No doubt he was already dying to get back to her, Kate reflected bitterly as Joss drove her home, if for no other reason than to relieve the ache that *thinking* about her while he was holding Kate in his arms had obviously engendered. Then she hated herself for her contemptible thoughts.

By the time Joss had driven them back to her house, an uncomfortable tension was filling the car.

Joss pulled into the drive, despite Kate's assertion that he could stop outside the house, and as he stopped the engine he said blandly, 'There's no need to worry, Kate. I'm not about to pounce on you.'

The derision in his voice stung, and she retorted quickly, 'I never thought you were.'

'Ah ... of course not. You're far too old to generate that kind of response.'

As he turned away from her, Kate suddenly realised how ridiculously she was behaving.

'I'm sorry,' she apologised, adding lamely, 'It's just that it's all been such a shock ...'

The unexpected sensation of his hand clasping hers warmly made her jump, but Joss seemed unaware of it.

'I'm sorry, too. Here I am, an adult, mature male of forty-odd,' he added ruefully, 'and for the life of me I can't seem to stop myself behaving like an immature fool. Well, the experience is a salutary one, if nothing else ...'

'Would you like to come in for a nightcap?' Kate asked, offering an olive branch, and then biting her lip savagely as she worried that he might misinterpret her invitation.

To her relief he did not, saying easily, 'That sounds a good idea; there are still one or two things we ought to discuss. I don't want to pressure you into acting as my go-between with Sophy, Kate. If you've any qualms at all ...'

'No,' she told him quickly. 'In the circumstances, it's only fair that I should be the one to tell her.'

'Because she might not believe me?' he asked ironically as they walked towards the back door together. 'Well, in the circumstances, I could hardly blame her.'

As she started to make the coffee, the sight of him leaning against her kitchen units filling the room with his presence made her feel tensely on edge, until a thought struck her.

'If you're interested, I've got some photograph albums of Sophy...' she offered hesitantly.

Immediately a warm smile illuminated his face. 'I'd love to see them.'

'I'll go and get them,' Kate told him. 'You could be looking at them in the sitting-room while I make the coffee.'

As she hurried past him she missed the comprehensive, rather grim look he gave her as he noticed the way she was careful about not coming too close to him.

The albums were upstairs in her parents' wardrobe. Kate brought them down and put them in the sitting-room, leaving Joss to study them alone. Her father had been a keen amateur photographer, and he had insisted on keeping a record of Sophy's growing years as he had done her own. Joss was so deeply immersed in them that when she walked in with the coffee he was oblivious to her presence.

From behind him she could see the familiar photographs of her daughter... Sophy pigtailed and gap-toothed, riding her first proper bike, squinting into the sunshine... Sophy wrapped up in the bright red hat and gloves her mother had knitted for her, while the two of them built a snowman.

'She's very like you,' she offered tentatively.

He put down the album and turned round. 'And you were still able to love her?'

The dry irony in his voice made her flush a little. She wondered if he had guessed that, despite everything, she had never been able to teach herself to hate him, and that when Sophy was born her first feeling on discovering that she was the image of him had been of overwhelming joy.

'There's one here of the two of you together,' he said abruptly, flicking back to the beginning of the album. 'How old was she then?'

It was the photograph her father had taken of Sophy. She had been ten days old. She was sitting in the garden with her, the flowers providing a soft, colourful background.

'She was ten days old,' she told him. It was devastating how just looking at that photograph could bring back the emotions of that time . . . her overwhelming joy and pride in her child, her anxiety for her future . . . her own loneliness and confusion . . . her intense, unending longing for Joss to be with them.

'And you were sixteen,' he said savagely, closing the book. 'I deserved to be shot. If anyone had done to Sophy what I did to you . . . I think I'd have wanted to destroy him. Is that how your father felt about me, Kate?'

She shook her head.

'No. He wasn't like that. He was very gentle . . . very compassionate. He wanted to make it easy for me to go on with my life, I suspect, and so he said that there were times when we all did things we would later regret and feel ashamed of.

That was one of the arguments he used to stop me trying to find you,' she added wryly, missing the curious flare of emotion in Joss's eyes.

'You *wanted* to find me?'

'At first. I was so frightened, you see... I loved you... or I thought I did.' She bit her lip. 'I don't suppose I knew what love was, really, but Dad made me see that if I did succeed in finding you, I would be causing your wife terrible unhappiness. That made me stop and think. He was trying to make me see that there were other things involved than my own feelings...'

'He sounds a very caring man,' Joss said abruptly.

'He was,' Kate agreed. 'They both were... him and Mum. Please don't feel too bad, Joss,' she added huskily, reaching out instinctively to cover his wrist with her hand in a gesture of reassurance. 'Mum and Dad were marvellous to both me and Sophy. Dad retired early and he spent a lot of time with her. More time I'm sure than many fathers are able to spend with their children. She never suffered any lack...'

'Of a father,' Joss put in savagely. 'No, I'm sure she didn't. In fact, to judge from what you're saying to me, she did far better without me in her life. A loving mother... devoted grandparents... security and grace her gifts from all three of you. No, I'm damn sure *she* didn't feel any lack.'

He sounded so angry that Kate stared curiously at him.

'But what about *me*, Kate?' he continued bitterly. '*I* was not so fortunate. I... there was nothing in my life to compensate for what I might have shared with her...'

Surprised by his vehemence, Kate said uncertainly, 'But you've been free to marry, to have children...'

'So I have. Unfortunately things didn't work out that way. My wife didn't want a family. Children had no place in her life, and rather than give me any, she divorced me.'

'You could have married again,' Kate said helplessly.

Joss gave a mirthless laugh.

'Is that really how you see me—as a man who, having once made such a traumatic mistake, could easily and carelessly attempt that kind of commitment a second time? You aren't the only one to carry scars from our relationship, you know, Kate,' he told her more quietly. 'It took me one hell of a long time to get over the fact that you'd ditched me. By the time I had I was thirty...the kind of watershed in a man's life when he starts thinking seriously about his future.

'I thought about mine and I married. That was a mistake. And it isn't one I want to repeat.' He lifted the album on to the sofa and stood up.

'I think I'll pass on the coffee, if you don't mind,' he said tiredly. 'I've got an early start in the morning.'

Silently Kate walked with him to the back door.

'Thank you for...for a very pleasant evening,' she said awkwardly as he turned towards her.

The light from the kitchen illuminated the hard structure of his bones, the shadows cast by the porch adding depth to the slant of his cheekbones, so that for a moment he looked almost gaunt.

'Pleasant.' His voice was dry and cynical. 'What a liar you are, Kate; you hated every moment of it—and some moments more than others,' he added sardonically.

He walked to his car without another word, and Kate stood by the door until he had driven off, thinking that it was a miracle that he hadn't guessed the truth. She hadn't hated the evening at all. She had just been petrified of somehow betraying to him the fact that she found it impossible to forget that once she had lain in his arms and made love with him, and that that loving had been the most intensely pleasurable experience of her life, and that it was because of *that* that she hadn't felt the slightest attraction for any other man. Because she had felt, somewhere deep inside her, that no other man would be able to make her feel the way *he* had been able to make her feel.

Sighing faintly, she closed the door and went inside. There were a lot of things she was going to have to do, if she was going to be able to go to London and see Sophy. Tomorrow she'd better start making plans.

CHAPTER SIX

'YOU'RE coming to London for the weekend...Mum, that's marvellous! We'd offer to put you up at the flat, but we've only got the one bedroom.'

Kate forced herself to smile into the receiver, not wanting Sophy to suspect that her visit was anything other than a spur of the moment decision, until she was able to be with her and explain everything to her in person.

'Still, you can come round on Friday to the flat, and then we can take you out for dinner on Saturday evening. How long will you be staying? *Where* will you be staying?'

'I'm not sure yet,' Kate told her quite truthfully, because Joss had simply said to leave everything to him, and she had no idea what hotel he was going to book her into. One that was not too expensive, she hoped.

They spent another half-hour talking about the wedding and the honeymoon. Sophy sounded deliriously happy and Kate crossed her fingers as she replaced the receiver, praying that the news she had for her would not prove too traumatic.

How would Sophy react to the discovery that John's mother's cousin was her father? Would she resent him because he had not been a part of her growing up, or would she perhaps resent and blame *her* because she had brought her up in ignorance of the truth?

Luckily they did not have too many bookings for the weekend, and Lucy was quite happy to cope on her own. Kate had booked herself a seat on the train, and had telephoned the private number Joss had given her to tell him what time it would be arriving.

It had been disappointing to discover that she was speaking into an answering machine. Where had Joss been? Out with his red-headed secretary? His private life was no concern of hers, she reminded herself as she replaced the receiver, her stomach churning tensely at the thought of the weekend to come.

To make matters worse, she had a disastrous week. On Wednesday she had a puncture when she was driving home from cooking and serving an executive lunch at some offices in York, which necessitated her having to unload the car to get at the spare wheel.

The road was a fairly lonely one, and she was very glad to have the wheel changed and the car back on the road after she had been subjected to a variety of comments from passing drivers.

The men calling out to her probably meant no harm, but these days, when there was so much violence against women, she felt uncomfortably vulnerable until she was on the move again.

On Thursday morning there was a power cut just when she was in the middle of baking and freezing a variety of their stock dishes, and on Thursday evening, just before she set out with the food for a very important and lavish silver-wedding party, she had a telephone call from one of the part-timers who helped them with the serving and clearing up on such occasions to say that she wasn't well and wouldn't be able to work as planned that evening.

A frantic ring round their other part-timers failed to produce someone to take her place, and, knowing that Lucy was going to be working almost all weekend, Kate heroically refused her offer of help and insisted that she would be able to manage.

She did—just—and it was almost four o'clock in the morning when she eventually managed to crawl into bed.

The jangling of her alarm just after ten made her groan and reach instinctively to silence its imperative call until she realised what day it was.

Cursing mildly under her breath, she got up and had a quick, icy-cold shower, hoping it would stir her sluggish senses into something approaching life.

The sun was shining warmly outside. The only thing she had that was suitable for wearing in London was the silk dress she had bought for Sophy's wedding, which fortunately was simple enough not to shriek 'wedding'.

Having drunk a piping hot cup of coffee and thrown a few things into an overnight bag, she decided recklessly that, if she discovered she had forgotten something, then she would just have to buy a substitute while she was in London.

She just made it for the train, arriving at the station feeling hot and flustered, which wasn't like her at all, and as she sank down into her seat, relieved that she had taken the precaution of going

to the expense of booking it when she saw how busy
the train was, she acknowledged that a good ninety
per cent of her tension was not the result of her
frantically busy and disruptive week, but was
caused entirely by the thought of seeing Joss again.

As the train picked up speed, she tried to concentrate on how she was going to break the news
to Sophy. She would be shocked, of course, but
probably very thrilled as well, Kate acknowledged
a little wryly. Joss was a father any young woman
could be proud of, and he would be doubly precious
to Sophy, who had spent all her young life believing that *her* father wasn't worthy of her love or
respect.

Yes. Sophy would be thrilled, and probably a
little sad as well, when she thought of all the years
she and Joss could have shared and had not.
Already the tie between Sophy and herself had
weakened, first when she went away to university
and then later, when she went to London and met
John, and Kate knew that it was only natural that
this should be the case. Now she would be forced
to stand to one side and perhaps witness Sophy
forming a bond with her father from which she
would be excluded.

Logic warred with emotion as she tried to remind
herself that it would only be natural that both
Sophy and Joss should want to get to know one
another. After all, they shared a very special bond.
And with Joss in London, he would have far more
opportunity to see Sophy than she did herself.

She closed her eyes as she felt the tiny darting
spears of jealousy twist her insides.

What was she jealous of? Sharing Sophy with Joss ... or the intimacy which would quite naturally spring up between father and daughter and from which she would be excluded.

Her throat had gone dry and tight, and she was relieved when a girl came round with a trolley selling coffee and sandwiches, glad to have something else, however mundane, to focus her attention on.

She chose a sandwich, remembering that she hadn't had time for any breakfast, but after two mouthfuls, despite the fact that it was fresh and well-made, she found her stomach rolling protestingly so that she had to put it on one side.

To her own despair she recognised that it was the thought of seeing Joss again that was causing most of her anxiety, rather than the knowledge of what she had to tell Sophy.

She must stop thinking about him so obsessively, she told herself angrily. It was ridiculous, behaving like this, focusing all her thoughts and mental energies on him like an adolescent. Just because he had implied that his life had not been an emotionally happy one ... Just because he had been angry at her refusal to see herself as a desirable woman; that did not mean ...

Did not mean what? she asked herself bitterly. Did not mean that he found her attractive ... that he wished things had been different? Was she really idiotic enough to think it might? Surely she was old enough and sensible enough to accept that, while he might have regrets about the past, while he might quite naturally want to include Sophy in his life, that did not mean that he wished to include her in it?

As the train drew closer to London, she warned herself that she must not give in to ridiculous daydreams; she must not allow herself to be seduced by her own wishful thinking, imagining that he could still feel something for her. She shuddered a little, all too easily picturing in her own mind's eye the pathetic figure she could become if she gave in to the temptation to believe that miracles could happen, and that Joss could feel the same way about her as she did about him.

It had taken her such a dangerously brief space of time to fall in love with him all over again. She had thought herself incapable of experiencing such feelings... had thought herself too sensible, too mature, too worldly wise... and yet after just a few hours in his company she had been reacting just as violently and emotionally to him as she had done as a teenager. The same thudding heartbeats... the same frantic nervousness... the same sharp, physical pain of need.

It was unfair of fate to treat her like this, she reflected crossly as the train pulled into St Pancras. All around her people started to get up. She picked up her own bag, and inadvertently caught the eye of the businessman who had been seated opposite her.

He gave her an appreciative smile that made her flush a little, and as she turned quickly and awkwardly into the aisle she remembered Sophy saying to her only a few months ago, 'Whenever a man shows any interest in you, you freeze them off so hard I'm surprised they aren't turned to blocks of ice on the spot.'

She had denied Sophy's allegations, but now, as she followed the other passengers off the train, she wondered if there was after all some truth in it.

'It's almost as though you feel you *have* to deny your own sexuality,' Sophy had added musingly, with the frankness that Kate, with her different up-bringing and outlook, sometimes found disconcerting.

She had shaken her head, but Sophy had looked at her thoughtfully and said softly, 'I suppose it's because of having me...because you felt you'd done something wrong.'

Her comment had come too close to the truth for Kate to bear it with equanimity. It was true that she did carry a burden of guilt for having conceived Sophy outside marriage and with a man who had commitments to another woman and child. And it hadn't helped knowing that it had been *her* weakness, *her* love, *her* intense need that had ob-literated everything other than her need to be part of Joss in the most intimate way there was. She hadn't given a thought to the fact that she might conceive...hadn't even cared...had wanted only Joss's possession, Joss's lovemaking...Joss himself.

Well, she had soon learned the price of such wanton selfishness, and she had made sure that she never allowed herself to experience that kind of temptation again.

After Sophy's birth, she had wanted nothing from life other than the emotional safety of herself and her daughter.

She had, she recognised with a tiny shiver of perception, quite deliberately slammed and barred the door on her own sexuality; that door remained barred, and she had been quite content that it should be... until last weekend.

She stopped dead, oblivious to the irritation of other travellers who almost bumped into her as she forced herself to acknowledge that her increasing tension and sleepless nights all this week had been caused by the shock and apprehension of discovering that she was not, as she had comfortably supposed, totally indifferent to physical arousal; she was just very unfortunate in being one of those women who, while totally unaroused by the majority of men she met, had this intensely strong and deep-rooted responsiveness to one particular man.

It had stunned her that her desire for Joss should have surfaced so quickly and so devastatingly, almost as though the intervening years had never existed. Her feelings were more appropriate to a young girl than a mature woman, she remonstrated with herself, but in vain they refused to subside, and now here she was, standing in the middle of a busy train station, knowing that the safest thing for her to do was to put as much distance between herself and Joss as she could; instead of which, here she was in London, knowing that she was going to be spending at least part of the weekend with him, and knowing equally well that his interest in her was purely as Sophy's mother. Which only went to show that it was true that there was no fool like an old one, she admitted tiredly, pulling her thoughts into some kind of order, and heading reluctantly for the main concourse of the station.

Joss had said that he would send someone to meet her, and for some reason, once she was through the barrier, she started looking around for a striking redhead.

It was a slight shock therefore to be approached by a uniformed chauffeur, who it seemed had had no difficulty in recognising her, because he touched her lightly on the arm so that she whirled round, and then asked calmly, 'Miss Seton?'

Kate ducked her head in acknowledgement and was efficiently relieved of her overnight bag and gently escorted out into the sunlight and into the Jaguar saloon which she recognised as belonging to Joss.

Because the traffic was, to her, appallingly heavy and impatient, she refrained from addressing any comments to the chauffeur, not wanting to distract him from his driving.

Only the very central parts of London were in any way familiar to her. The only time she had visited Sophy and John's brand new apartment in the newly refurbished and very fashionable Dockside area John had picked her up from the station, and she felt very much like a country mouse in a very big and bewildering city as the chauffeur negotiated the Jaguar through the heavy traffic.

When he took an abrupt turn into a narrow street the tall buildings on either side enclosed it so much that Kate almost felt claustrophobic, and it was a relief when the car emerged into a small and almost quiet square.

Tall, early-Victorian houses surrounded the small iron-railed garden with its shadowing trees, and Kate did not need to look at the expensive cars parked outside the houses to recognise the square as a very expensive area.

As they drove down one side of the square she saw that the buildings all had discreet brass plaques outside, suggesting that most of them were now in use as offices rather than private homes, but she didn't realise until the chauffeur turned in between a pair of opening wrought-iron security gates that led to a private mews parking area that Joss's offices were housed in one of these elegant buildings.

For some reason she had supposed his offices would be in a very modern high-rise block. Perhaps she should have known better. She remembered that the young Joss had been very passionate indeed about preserving buildings of the past, and it was perhaps only natural that he should opt for offices in an old building rather than a modern one.

Tactfully she waited for the chauffeur to open her door for her, smiling a 'thank you' at him as he removed her bag from the boot.

She felt increasingly nervous, not just about meeting Joss, which was bad enough, but about meeting him on his own territory. Something about London seemed to sap her confidence and make her feel diminished. Perhaps it was the sight of so many eager, ambitious young faces...or perhaps it was just that she had lived in the country for too long.

Or perhaps it was the thought of meeting Joss on his own territory; a territory which he and Sophy shared and from which she was excluded.

A tiny shiver ran through her, and immediately the chauffeur frowned, saying quickly, 'It's this way. Sometimes the breeze round here out of the sun can be quite chilly.'

She wasn't used to being treated as though she was as fragile as a piece of spun glass . . . fragile and feminine, precious and loved . . . Will you stop this? she demanded angrily of herself as the chauffeur stopped to produce a key to unlock the white-painted rear door. Above it was a fanlight; not as imposing a fanlight as that surmounting the front door, but a very attractive fanlight none the less. The door had a number on it, and opened not, as she had anticipated, into a foyer or corridor such as one might associate with company offices, but into a small, square hallway, decorated more as one would expect a private home to be decorated.

A flight of stairs led upwards, carpeted in thick grey-blue Wilton.

'Up here,' the chauffeur directed her, indicating a discreetly concealed lift. 'Mr Bennett said to take you straight up.'

Straight up where? Kate wondered as the lift swept dizzyingly upwards and then rocked un-pleasantly to a halt. She had never liked high-speed lifts, and as she stepped out of this one she felt both light-headed and vaguely oppressed.

She was in another square hallway. This one had a very splendid arched window that overlooked the square and allowed light to spill into the hall and down the stairs.

There was only one door off the hall. The chauffeur produced another key and unlocked it, standing back respectfully for her to precede him.

Uncertainly she did so, tiny prickles of alarm feathering the tiny hairs on her skin as she found herself walking into a room that was most definitely not an office, but rather a very comfortable and private sitting-room-cum-study, complete with an imposing Victorian fireplace and a wall of mahogany library bookcases with a patina that made her catch her breath in envy and long to run her fingertips along their polished surface.

By the time she had resisted the impulse, the chauffeur had disappeared.

She glanced wildly around the room, and then walked uncertainly over to the window. She was right at the top of the building. Down below her, she could see people walking on the other side of the square. Two doors opened off the room she was in. She wondered nervously where they led, and where Joss was.

She didn't have to wait long to find out. While she was staring out of the window, she heard a door open and swung round tensely.

'Sorry I wasn't here to welcome you,' Joss said easily as he came into the room. 'A telephone call that went on rather longer than I'd planned. Coffee . . . or would you prefer me to show you to your room first?'

Her *room*? Kate stared at him and managed to ask huskily, 'I'm staying here?'

'I tried to book you into a hotel, but all the better ones were fully booked. Tourists ... I have a spare bedroom here, so I thought ... But of course if you'd prefer me to make some other arrangements ...'

He was watching her closely, and for some reason Kate felt as though she was being tested, but for what and why she had no idea.

It was ridiculous to feel uneasy at spending the weekend in what was obviously Joss's private flat; after all, it wasn't as though he was likely to try and seduce her. Far from it.

'The room has its own private bathroom ...'

'Are you sure I won't be in the way?' Kate asked uncertainly, unable to stop herself from remembering the way his secretary had clung possessively to his arm.

Joss frowned and then raised his eyebrows. 'Why should you be? *I* invited you to come down here, remember?'

'Yes, but only so that I could break the ice for you with Sophy ... I'm seeing her tonight at her flat for dinner. I thought that might be a good opportunity to tell her ... and then perhaps tomorrow I could bring her here to see you ...'

'Always supposing she'll want to see me.'

Kate had spent all week thinking about Sophy's reaction to what she had to tell her; privately she had few doubts that, after her initial shock, Sophy would want to meet her father ... as her *father* and not just as John's relative. She wanted to tell him so, but the words stuck in her throat, almost as though she begrudged him the knowledge that

Sophy wouldn't reject him. Why was that? Because she already felt jealous?

'You must be hungry,' he announced curtly. 'It's a bit late for lunch, but if it appeals to you I thought we might perhaps go somewhere for afternoon tea. The Ritz...'

Kate was just about to refuse his invitation, feeling quite sure that it was an invitation made purely out of politeness, when he added with a surprisingly boyish grin, 'It's something I've always wanted to try, but it's one of those things that a male definitely needs a female companion to indulge in without collecting odd looks.'

Kate almost said waspishly that she was sure that if that was the case he had had no need to wait for her to come along, and that she was quite sure there were any number of women who would jump at the chance of having afternoon tea with him, but she stopped herself and gave him a rather forced smile instead.

'That would be lovely. I am rather hungry, and Sophy suggested I join them for dinner at about eight.' She pulled a wry face. 'She thinks I'm spending the afternoon shopping. She was talking about asking John to arrange for us to go out for dinner somewhere tomorrow evening.'

'Well, if she does consent to come and see me tomorrow afternoon, I expect she'll be glad of the opportunity to spend the evening alone with you and John,' Joss said easily.

His sensitivity surprised Kate. She was not used to men who so quickly picked up on her thoughts and apprehensions, and she wasn't sure if she welcomed his ability to do so. It made her feel edgy and vulnerable.

'You must have work to do,' she said lamely, suddenly alarmed at spending time alone with him, frightened of what she might betray.

'Nothing that won't wait. The company has now reached the stage where I have a very competent staff and can quite easily delegate.'

'It must be convenient for you living here... above your offices.'

'Convenient, yes... but this place was never intended to be anything more than a *pied-à-terre*. It's somewhere to sleep and eat, but it isn't a home, and I've reached that stage in my life where I want a home.

'In fact, I'm planning to move out to the country. Dorset. I've bought a property there... a vicarage with a couple of acres of land. It's liveable-in— just. With the new advanced computer systems that are available, I'll be able to live and work from there, and keep in touch with my personnel here.'

'Won't you miss London?' Kate asked him curiously.

He shook his head. 'No. Not now. You must come to Dorset and see the house. I could do with a woman's advice on décor and furnishings.'

Kate stared at him, sure that he was merely making conversation, not daring to allow herself to believe that he actually meant her to take the invitation seriously. Flustered and uncomfortable with her own unruly reactions to him, she said awkwardly, 'Well, I expect Sophy will be delighted to help you. She has a real flair for that kind of thing. You should see their apartment...'

She thought she heard Joss give a faint sigh, but she had turned away from him and did not dare turn round to look at him. Every time she looked into his eyes she went almost weak at the knees, a ridiculous reaction in a woman who was supposedly mature.

'I... I think I'd better tidy up a bit if we're going to the Ritz.'

'Your room's this way,' Joss informed her, crossing the room and opening one of the doors into a small corridor.

Two doors opened off it. He opened one of them and held the door for her to precede him into the room.

It was a pleasantly large-sized bedroom, with a double bed, a large wardrobe, an easy chair and a writing-desk, decorated in muted shades of terracotta and blue. Kate had no doubt that everything in it was very expensive, and had been chosen with care and an eye for detail, but the room lacked soul. It was more like a hotel bedroom than a bedroom in a private home, she reflected sadly as she stared around it.

And not for the first time she felt a tiny shaft of pity for Joss.

'Bathroom's through here,' he told her, indicating another door. 'The other room off this corridor is my bedroom. Kitchen-cum-dining-room's on the other side of the sitting-room.'

Her case was already in her room, and Joss glanced at his watch and said casually, 'Ten minutes be long enough?'

Kate nodded.

Once she was alone in the room, she moved round it uncertainly. The last thing she had expected was that she would be staying with Joss, and her heart started to beat with fierce excitement which she sternly tried to quell, reminding herself that in the circumstances it was the most sensible course, and that for her to read anything personal into his decision was to court unhappiness.

A quick look in the bedroom mirror assured her that her make-up was still intact, and, removing her toilet bag from her overnight case, she went into the bathroom.

The brilliant lights focused on the mirrored walls dazzled her for a moment. The bathroom was elegantly opulent, decorated in the same restrained terracotta and blue colours as the bedroom, but once again it lacked warmth and intimacy. It might have been the bathroom in a very upmarket and expensive hotel, rather than a private home.

Her hands stilled as she brushed her hair. There had been something bleak and heart-rending in Joss's expression when he told her that he had no home. She wondered what the house he had bought was like, and fought against allowing herself to feel excited and flattered at his invitation to go and see it. She really must stop taking everything he said to her personally, she derided herself, as she renewed her lipstick and then stepped back from the mirror, making a rueful face at her own reflection.

The silk dress was elegant and easy to wear, her arms slim and tanned beneath the short cap sleeves.

It really was time she found a more suitable hair-style, she decided, frowning at the unruly mass of thick blonde curls.

Her ten minutes was up, and she hurried back into the bedroom, picking up her jacket and opening the bedroom door.

As she opened the door into the sitting-room she could hear Joss talking to someone, but it was too late for her to withdraw. Joss was standing with his back to her, demanding almost curtly, 'Are you sure this isn't something you can handle?'

And standing at his side, eyeing Kate with dismissive contempt, stood his secretary.

'Hardly, Joss. You know that Mac Phillips prefers to deal personally with you.'

Joss was frowning as he turned round and saw Kate. 'I'm sorry, Kate,' he apologised tersely. 'Something's come up that I have to deal with, and I'm afraid I'm going to have to forgo the Ritz.'

Over the years Kate had become adept at the use of camouflage to hide her real feelings. It hadn't always been easy being a single parent in the days when to be an unmarried mother was not considered either fashionable or appropriate.

She summoned the smile she had perfected in those early days, an easy, protective widening of her lips that didn't reach her eyes, her voice cool and reasonable as she assured him that she didn't mind.

Lucille, his secretary, was now standing behind Joss, and Kate watched as the other woman gave her a triumphant, malicious smile. Lucille was jealous of her. Kate subdued a bitter desire to laugh. If only the other woman knew.

'I'll just get his file. It's in my bedroom. I was reading it the other night. I am sorry about this, Kate,' Joss apologised again, still frowning. 'I can't understand why he should be ringing today when I'm seeing him next week.'

Out of the corner of her eye Kate saw the tiny twitch Lucille gave as Joss left them, and she wondered if the redhead knew how much her body language was betraying.

The moment the door had closed behind Joss, she turned on Kate and said warningly, 'Don't read too much into this invitation of Joss's, will you? He's a sucker for lame ducks and, after all, he could hardly refuse to let you stay here when you'd virtually invited yourself to do so.'

Where originally Kate had found herself slightly intimidated by the other woman's elegance and sophistication, now a sudden spurt of anger came to her rescue and she was able to challenge quietly, 'Is that what Joss told you? That I invited myself here?'

A thin tide of angry colour darkened Lucille's skin.

'Not directly,' she admitted with a tiny shrug. 'But it's obvious what happened.'

She might think so, but it was plain to Kate that she had no idea of the real reason for her visit, and that cheered her. Joss had described Lucille as his personal secretary, and Kate had realised from everything he had said to her, that the intimacy she thought she had seen between them during the reception had been misleading.

Apparently it had, but Lucille was plainly trying to warn her off Joss.

Only a woman who was desperately insecure resorted to such tactics, Kate acknowledged when Joss came back, still frowning.

'I shouldn't be more than half an hour or so——' he began, but Lucille interrupted him, saying quickly,

'Oh, Joss, I forgot. The estimates for the Harwood contract are ready, and you said you wanted to go through them as quickly as possible.'

'Don't worry,' Kate said calmly, smiling at them both. 'I've got some shopping to do.'

It was a lie but she was too proud to allow Joss to think that she was dependent on him in any way.

He didn't seem as relieved by her claim as she had expected.

'How long will you be gone?' he demanded tersely.

Kate shook her head. 'I don't know. Two hours . . . maybe three.'

His mouth tightened, as though her response had displeased him. He gave her a brief, indecipherable look, and then glanced at the papers in his hand, almost as though he resented the fact that they were taking him away from her.

Fool, she mocked herself, after Joss had given her two keys to let herself back into the apartment. He was probably only too relieved to be spared the boredom of entertaining her.

CHAPTER SEVEN

SOME stubborn impulse Kate didn't really want to admit to kept her out much longer than she had said and, sitting in a small café she had found, she decided that, rather than go back to Joss's apartment and face the possibility of being confronted a second time by Lucille's jealous resentment, she might as well go straight to Sophy and John's.

She wiled away the intervening time window-shopping and then having a light snack in another café, before giving in to the extravagance of taking a taxi to Sophy's.

In the event, because of the traffic, she was not much earlier than they had arranged.

The apartment Sophy and John had bought in a brand new Dockside development was familiar to Kate from an earlier visit, but once again she couldn't help marvelling at the way the old building had been converted and the whole area turned into a highly desirable residential district.

Sophy and John's apartment complex included a large private sports centre complete with swimming pool. A whole rash of new and very up-market shops selling everything from home-made French bread to every type of exotic fruit and vegetable imaginable gave testimony to the wealth and life-style of the inhabitants of the area.

Sophy answered the door to Kate's knock, almost dragging her inside and hugging her enthusiastically. Both she and John were sun-tanned from their honeymoon, and Kate reflected as she looked at her daughter that she had never seen her looking so well and happy.

'I'm sorry I'm a bit early...'

'Don't be,' Sophy told her firmly. 'Let's go into the sitting-room and have a glass of wine. We thought we'd get a take-away later, but we haven't ordered anything because we weren't sure what you'd fancy. There are three or four places near here.'

'I'm not hungry at the moment,' Kate told her, accepting the glass of chilled wine John poured for her, and following Sophy out on to the large terrace that overlooked the river.

'Where are you staying?' Sophy asked conversationally, as John disappeared into the kitchen to fill her glass and his own.

Kate took a deep breath. She had gone over and over in her mind all week how best to introduce the purpose of her visit, and now suddenly she knew that the simplest way was to tell the truth.

'I'm staying with Joss Bennett,' she said as casually as she could.

The effect on Sophy was immediate and electric.

'John's mother's cousin!' Her mouth dropped as she stared at her mother. 'But, Ma...'

John had returned with their own drinks and looked as confused as Sophy.

'Sophy, there's something I have to tell you,' she said quietly, reaching out to touch her daughter's arm There was no easy way to do this. 'Joss Bennett is your father.'

She bit her lip as she saw the colour drain from Sophy's face, but, much as she ached to hold her, she forced herself not to move as John went quickly to Sophy's side and held her tightly.

'I'm sorry. I know it's a shock, but there's no easy way to tell you any of this.'

'*Joss* is my father. But you told me that my father was a married man with a family,' Sophy accused shakily.

'Yes, I know. And that's exactly what I thought he was...' She took a steadying breath. 'I think it might be easier if I started at the beginning.'

Quietly she did so, relating the course of events as both she and Joss now realised they must have happened.

'So Joss's landlady deliberately lied to you...deliberately lied to you *both*... How could she do that?'

'She didn't know I was pregnant,' Kate told her. 'I didn't even know it myself at the time. It was quite a shock to find out what must have happened after all these years.'

'Yes, it must have been,' Sophy agreed soberly. 'And I suppose if Joss...my father...' she stumbled a little over the words, but Kate saw, with a sudden sharp pang, that beneath her shock Sophy was already beginning to adjust to the reality of Joss as her father '...hadn't turned up at the wedding, you'd never have known.'

'Very probably,' Kate agreed. 'He came to see me the weekend after the wedding, because he'd realised from what John's mother had told him about us that you must be his child. He thought I'd deliberately kept you from him . . . and that was how the truth came out that both of us had been deceived.' She stretched out her hand to cover her daughter's. 'He wants to meet you, Sophy . . . to get to know you. I promised I'd break the news to you. He doesn't want to force the relationship on you.'

Out of the corner of her eye she saw the quick look Sophy gave John, and the reassuring way he squeezed her hand.

'And would you mind, Ma . . . if . . . if I did see him?'

She forced herself to smile warmly and fib, 'Of course not. He *is* your father, after all, and I feel guilty at having deprived you of him all these years . . .'

That at least was the truth.

Instantly Sophy reassured her. 'But you didn't know! You did what seemed to be best.'

'He's invited you and John round to his apartment tomorrow. It will give the two of you a chance to talk properly,' Kate told her jerkily, her emotions threatening to get out of control.

'I suppose he didn't want to approach me directly in case you were upset,' Sophy mused, obviously following her own train of thought, her eyes suddenly sparkling mischievously as she began to get over her shock. 'Wouldn't it be wonderful if the two of you were to fall in love all over again and——'

'That's hardly likely, Sophy,' Kate interrupted her curtly, so curtly in fact that Sophy frowned at her curiously.

'You don't still hate him do you, Mum?' she asked uncertainly. 'I know that he hurt you terribly, but it wasn't his fault and...'

Hate him? She had *never* hated him, Kate acknowledged angrily.

'No, of course I don't,' she reassured Sophy, and then added more gently, 'Perhaps I over-reacted a little. I know you were only joking and that you know how embarrassing it would be both for your father and for me if people started linking us together.'

Sophy was frowning.

'Embarrassing—why? Both of you are free and over eighteen! What could be embarrassing about it? Unless... are you worried that they might guess that Joss is my father?'

Kate blinked. She hadn't got as far as worrying about that, but now it struck her that if Joss was going to acknowledge Sophy publicly as his child it would mean acknowledging her own past role in his life. How was she going to feel about John's family and her own friends knowing who Joss was?

'Sophy, I'm thirty-seven years old,' she reminded her daughter stiffly. 'Naturally Joss would feel embarrassed if people were to start assuming there's some kind of romantic link between us.'

'What?' Sophy exploded indignantly. 'Baloney! For heaven's sake, Ma, you're *thirty*-seven, not eighty-seven!'

'Lucille is thirty, if that,' Kate pointed out rawly, her face flaming brilliantly as she recognised how much she might have betrayed, but although John gave her a quick, keen look Sophy was fortunately too caught up in her own emotions to notice her mother's slip.

'And looks a good deal older! Anyway, age isn't important. It's the person you are that matters. You loved one another once.'

'We *thought* we did, Sophy,' Kate corrected wryly. 'I was barely sixteen and Joss only five years older and, no matter what we might have thought we felt at the time, neither of us was really anywhere near mature enough to call those feelings love.'

She reached out and touched Sophy's arm gently.

'For your sake I'm glad that all this has happened, and that it's giving you a chance to get to know your father, albeit rather late in your life, but the relationship you'll have with him will of necessity be separate from the relationship you have with me...'

'Like a parcel passed between two divorced parents,' Sophy scoffed acidly. 'At least as a child I was spared *that*.' She saw Kate's face and hugged her impulsively. 'Oh, Ma, I'm sorry. I had a wonderful childhood, and if you think I'm blaming you in any way because my father wasn't a part of that childhood, then don't.' She hesitated, and then asked almost nervously, 'Are you really sure you don't mind if I see him?'

Mind...of course she minded, but in so many complex ways that she could barely understand them all herself, and so she sidestepped the question and said instead, 'He's your father, Sophy. It's only natural that you should want to know him and that he should want to know you.'

It was a very emotional evening, with John manfully trying to keep them all on an even keel.

'Just wait until Mother hears about this,' he commented, when Sophy had had a little weep and implored Kate for the umpteenth time to tell her if she minded if she saw Joss. In the end they spent the entire evening talking about what had happened, and the sheer coincidence of it happening at all.

It was late when Kate finally got up to leave, having arranged that both John and Sophy would come round to Joss's apartment early the following afternoon.

'I'll drive you back, if you like,' John offered, but Kate shook her head.

'There's no need,' she reassured him. 'I'll get a taxi.'

While John rang for one, Sophy whispered dazedly, 'I still can't take it in. I feel like a kid who's suddenly discovered Father Christmas has been in the middle of the summer, thrilled to bits and yet half expecting it's all going to disappear again.'

'It won't,' Kate assured her firmly, as they hugged one another.

*   *   *

On the way back in the taxi she wondered how Joss had spent the evening. Sophy must have been on his mind. He must have been worrying...wondering...and suddenly she was anxious to be with him, to reassure him that he need have no fears of Sophy rejecting him.

Her own fear of trespassing too intimately on the neutral ground between them, of embarrassing him with a warmth of emotion he could not want, were forgotten in her sudden urgent eagerness to assure him that Sophy was eager and willing to welcome him into her life.

Her own fears, her subconscious feeling that somehow he would come between Sophy and herself, were submerged in the vast, warm swell of emotion that rose up inside her and reached out towards him.

She glanced upwards towards the top of the building as she directed the taxi to stop, but could see no lights shining.

Did that mean that Joss was out? Absurd to feel so disappointed. After all, the news she had for him would quite easily keep until morning. So why did she have this let-down feeling...this sense of something almost approaching betrayal?

Paying off the taxi, she headed for the rear entrance to the building, relieved to see that it was well-illuminated; she felt all the country dweller's nervousness at the thought of the dangers of the city late at night, but no one appeared as she unlocked the door and let herself inside the ground-floor hallway.

She rejected the lift in favour of the stairs, and then wished she hadn't as she reached the top with a stitch in her side and her breathing uneven.

When she let herself into Joss's apartment the sitting-room was in darkness. Joss was obviously out, she acknowledged dejectedly as she switched on the lights and removed her jacket.

With Lucille? She hated the way her heart thudded so painfully at the thought. Her throat felt dry and she was longing for a cup of tea.

She couldn't wait up for Joss to return, of course, she acknowledged as she found her way to the kitchen and filled the kettle. The kitchen's grey and white décor struck her as very cold and cheerless, even though it was undoubtedly very streamlined and fashionable.

She wouldn't have swapped it for her own homely and rather shabby kitchen at home, she decided as she studied the small, hi-tech room.

Engrossed in her thoughts, she didn't hear the door open, and jumped visibly when she heard Joss say her name in a harshly curt voice.

Putting her hand on her chest, she gasped out loud and whirled round.

'Oh, Joss! You frightened me. I thought you were out.'

'Are you all right?' he asked her fiercely, ignoring her comment.

'All right?' She wasn't sure what he meant.

'You're breathing heavily, as though you've been running. London isn't exactly the safest place these days for a woman on her own.'

'I'm out of breath because I walked up the stairs instead of using the lift,' she told him quickly, but the stern look carving his mouth didn't relax, and all at once she felt almost like a little girl facing an angry parent.

'Why didn't you come back this afternoon?' he asked tersely.

Kate stared at him, nonplussed, not wanting to give him the real reason she had opted to go straight to Sophy's—that being the fact that she hadn't wanted to risk another meeting with Lucille.

'I... I didn't want to disturb you,' she fibbed wildly. 'I thought you might be busy... It's enough of an imposition for you that I'm here at all——'

'An imposition,' he pounced, his frown growing heavier. 'Don't be ridiculous. If anyone's being imposed upon, it's you. I was...' There was a small silence and then he said grimly, 'I suppose it never occurred to you that I might be worried when you didn't return?'

Kate's eyes widened. It hadn't. She was so used to living and being alone that it hadn't occurred to her at all.

'You could have rung me at Sophy's,' she told him reasonably, remembering that she had given him Sophy's number.

'Could I?' His voice was unfamiliarly harsh. 'And what if something *had* happened to you? What if you'd changed your mind and gone home? For goodness' sake, Kate. The arrangement was that you would come back here.'

Kate examined his taut features slowly. Was his concern genuinely for her, or for his relationship with Sophy? Had he suspected that she might have reneged on their agreement?

She gave him a cool smile.

'I'm a grown woman, Joss, and probably as unused as you are yourself to accounting to anyone for my movements. I'm sorry if you were... concerned.'

'Concerned?'

The look he gave her smashed through the cool barrier she was trying to erect to distance herself from him. Before she knew what was happening, he had taken hold of her, his fingers gripping her upper arms as he practically lifted her off her feet and shook her.

'Concerned? Damn you, Kate, I was practically out of my mind with fear.'

She could hardly breathe for the panic engulfing her... not that he might hurt her, but that her unruly body might betray her completely by advertising how easily she was aroused by the scent and heat of him... by the sheer male proximity of him; so much so that it was making her feel light-headed and dizzy.

She made a soft sound of protest in her throat, and instantly Joss released her, his face unusually pale in the too harsh glare of the kitchen lights.

'I'm sorry,' he said tersely. 'Did I hurt you? I'd forgotten how fragile you are. Bones like a bird's, tiny...' His fingers circled her wrist as though he was measuring its circumference, an abstracted absent gesture really, but one that made her flesh burn as though it was circled by fire.

Desperately she pulled away, the tension in the small kitchen almost a physical pressure tightening her skin.

Apprehension and excitement spiralled through her, twisting together to make one tight cord of sensation.

'I'm sorry if you were worried,' she apologised light-headedly. 'But there was no need. I'm an adult and perfectly capable of taking care of myself.'

She had said the wrong thing. His face tightened and so did his grip on her wrist.

'Completely self-sufficient. But not in every way, Kate. There are still some things that need the participation of another person—like this...'

She knew that he was going to kiss her, but even knowing it did nothing to avoid the downward descent of his mouth, nor its hungry settling against her own.

She could feel anger, pain and relief emanating from him; familiar sensations, which softened her defences and made her want to reassure him.

Her hand touched his face, smoothing the rough flesh of his jaw—and finding the rasping prickle of his beard.

Once, long ago, she had touched him like this, feathering shy fingers over his jaw and then tracing the line above his upper lip where he shaved—a dangerous and heady exploration for a girl who had never even been kissed properly before she met him. He had seemed so male...so powerful...so adult and far removed for her.

He had teased her fingertips with his tongue and then his teeth, nibbling delicately at them until she had been quivering with a pleasure she hadn't known existed.

Lost in the past, she was abruptly aware of tears smarting in her eyes. Then he had kissed her with tenderness and care; now he was kissing her with anger and dislike, and her comfort was the last thing he wanted.

As she lifted her hand from his face, he caught hold of her wrist. The pressure of his hard kiss slackened and he turned his mouth into the palm of her hand, caressing the soft flesh almost gently.

She had closed her eyes automatically when he'd started kissing her. Now she opened them and saw the dark fan of his lashes lying against his skin as his mouth moved delicately against her palm. He looked so vulnerable . . . so . . .

His lashes lifted and he looked at her, his eyes darkening shockingly as he saw that her own were filled with tears.

'Kate, I'm sorry. I hurt you . . . I didn't mean to. I was just so damned scared when you didn't come back,' he groaned.

And it was out of that fear and anger that he had kissed her, Kate recognised sadly, gently tugging her wrist free and stepping back from him.

'This is a difficult and emotional time for all of us,' she said huskily. 'I expect it's only natural that . . . that we're going to say and do things that would normally be out of character. You didn't hurt me, Joss. I could have moved . . . avoided you . . . your kiss . . .'

'But you didn't,' he said slowly. 'Why?'

There was something that had to be established between them so clearly that it would never be questioned, and now was the ideal time.

Taking a deep breath, she said quickly, 'Because, in the circumstances, I think we can both accept that we should feel a little... curiosity about one another...as people do when they've been...close and then meet again in later life. Normally there are barriers between them that make sure that curiosity is controlled. They're both normally married, or involved in other relationships. That...that doesn't seem to be the case here, and ...and I think that, while we both realise that it isn't possible to go back to the past...tonight...with emotions running high...'

'I gave way to my baser instincts and behaved as though we were still *in* the past and I'd every right to kiss you,' Joss finished for her, stunning her, because that wasn't what she'd meant at all. All she'd wanted to do was to assure him that she wasn't going to misunderstand his reasons for kissing her and that he wouldn't be embarrassed by her reading more into the embrace than there was.

She told him so, quickly, almost stammering in her haste to get the words out, not daring to look at him until she'd finished, and then surprising such a look of bitterness in his eyes that she stepped back from him automatically.

'You're very altruistic...or are you, Kate? Perhaps this is some kind of subtle warning disguised as concern, a warning not to try to intrude into your life because you don't want me there.'

He was making a statement, not asking a question, but Kate was too dumb with shock to respond anyway.

'If so, you're going to have to teach your body to fall into line with your brain,' he told her harshly, and as his glance slid deliberately down to the swell of her breasts Kate flinched to see the betraying outline of her distended nipples pushing against her silk dress.

It was an effort of will not to cross her hands protectively in front of her body. All desire for a cup of tea was gone. All she wanted now was to escape from Joss.

'It's late,' she told him, half gabbling the words. 'I think I'd better go to bed.' And then, as she hurried past him towards the door, she stopped and turned round, guilty colour staining her skin as she remembered what she had not yet told him.

'Sophy was...thrilled to learn that you're her father,' she told him nervously. 'She was shocked at first, of course...but once I'd explained... She and John are going to come round tomorrow as we discussed. Sophy did mention how surprised John's parents were going to be, and I realised that we hadn't talked about how public you wanted to make your relationship with her.'

He looked at her broodingly, as though she had angered him in some way.

'I don't care who knows that Sophy is my child,' he told her flatly. 'Why should I?'

His eyes challenged her and she gulped nervously.

'Well, no reason, only this afternoon Lucille seemed not to know why I was here.'

'She doesn't. It's true that I don't care who knows about Sophy, but until she had agreed to see me I felt honour-bound to keep our relationship private. In due course, Lucille, as my personal assistant, will have to be told about Sophy...'

'Your personal assistant...I thought the relationship between the two of you was rather more...intimate than that.'

Oh, lord, what was she saying? No wonder Joss was looking at her like that.

'You what?'

'It's no business of mine, of course,' she pressed on doggedly, realising she had come too far now to back down, 'but if Lucille is going one day to be Sophy's stepmother...'

Joss made a sound under his breath that made her flinch.

'Her stepmother? What the devil gave you that idea? I've already told you I am not sleeping with Lucille, never have slept with her and have no plans to sleep with her, let alone marry her. In point of fact,' he added dangerously, 'I haven't slept with a woman...any woman since my marriage broke up.

'I appreciate that in your eagerness to keep me well and truly out of your life, my marrying Lucille would appeal to you. But it doesn't appeal to *me*.'

Unable to say a word, Kate opened the door and fled, and not until she was safely tucked up in her solitary double bed did she allow herself to dwell on exactly why she should be feeling so deliriously pleased that Joss was not involved with Lucille.

Did she really need to ask herself? Hadn't she known from the moment she saw him again that nothing had changed...that despite her age and maturity she was no more proof against loving him now than she had been at sixteen?

The difference was that now she recognised the implausibility of that love being returned.

CHAPTER EIGHT

SOPHY and John were due to arrive at two, and after a telephone call from John to say that they were on their way Kate said quickly to Joss, 'I think it might be a good idea if I wasn't here. My presence will inhibit you both.' She bit down hard on her bottom lip to stop it trembling. This was one of the hardest things she had ever done, but she owed it to both of them. They needed the opportunity to reach out to one another without being afraid of hurting her.

'I'll go and do some window-shopping.'

'If that's what you want,' Joss told her harshly, his mouth compressing.

Surely he didn't *want* her here? She had done what she had said, had broken the news to Sophy. He must surely want now to be with her, without Kate hovering at their sides.

Instead of being grateful to her, though, he was behaving as though she had somehow betrayed him. She had thought that he would welcome the opportunity to get to know Sophy on his own. It seemed that she was wrong. He was standing with his back to her staring out of the window, his stance almost one of defeat.

'Please stay, Kate,' he begged gruffly, without looking at her. 'I'm so damned scared I might say or do the wrong thing.' He turned round, pushing irate fingers through his hair in a gesture of open uncertainty. 'I need you to be here, Kate.'

He needed *her* ...

'We both need you to be here,' he added quietly. 'Don't you see—you're the only real link between us? The only bridge.'

'But you're her father.'

'I'm a stranger,' Joss contradicted her flatly, and in his face Kate read both pain and anger. Even though she knew she was not to blame for the fact that he had never known about Sophy until now, she found herself weakening. She wanted to be there. She wanted to be a part of what was happening and not excluded from it.

'I've never been so damned scared in my life,' Joss burst out unexpectedly. 'What did you say when you told her, Kate? How did she react?'

She could hear the yearning in his voice and the force of her own jealousy shocked her. Jealous, of her own daughter. It was ridiculous.

She struggled to subdue her own feelings and responded quickly, 'She was shocked, of course...but excited. She wants to see you very much.'

She watched as hope and wariness struggled for supremacy, watching the subtle shifting of expressions crossing her face, and impulsively she reached out and placed her hand on his arm, saying reassuringly, 'She won't reject you, Joss. Remember this is as difficult for her as it is for you.'

'Not quite,' he told her with a wry grimace. 'She's my child and I already love her. She may not feel the same way about me,' he added bluntly. 'Love isn't always reciprocated.'

A statement of fact, or a subtle warning that he had guessed that her own adolescent feelings for him had been reactivated?

Her hand was still resting on his arm and she started to remove it, but Joss stopped her, taking hold of it and gripping it tightly.

'I haven't thanked you yet for everything you've done, Kate. Nor apologised for last night. I over-reacted... I was worried about you. I'm sorry.'

He bent his head, and she thought he was going to kiss her cheek lightly in a gesture of apology and friendship, but his free hand cupped her face and turned it.

'Can I kiss you?' he whispered against her mouth. 'For good luck.'

If it had been anyone else but Joss she would have refused, with a smile to soften the refusal, but because it *was* Joss, and because when she was with him she seemed unable to behave in her normal mature, sensible fashion, she nodded briefly, her lips parting on a soft sigh as his mouth moved gently against them.

The need to be close to him was so overwhelming that she obeyed it instinctively, closing the small gap between their bodies, making a soft sound of pleasure deep in her throat as she felt the warmth and strength of his body against her own.

His arms were round her, holding her so tightly that she could hardly breathe, his hands shaping her back, her waist and then the curves of her hips as the kiss deepened into urgent desire.

Her own hands lifted to his shoulders, then found the thick darkness of his hair and gloried in the soft silky feel of it. Her breasts swelled and ached, and she could feel a familiar sensation uncurling in her belly. She moved restlessly against him, a feminine provocation she wasn't even aware of making until she caught the smothered groan that convulsed his throat and felt him manoeuvre her so that her legs parted to admit the hard, muscled length of one of his, while his hands moved restlessly against her hips, urging her to repeat that tiny provocative movement.

It was the knowledge that he was aroused and that she was the cause of that arousal that shocked her into pulling away, her eyes betraying her shocked confusion as she looked up into his face and then away again, her own skin burning with hot colour as she saw the dark tide of arousal sweep his skin.

'You looked at me like that the first time I touched you here,' he told her thickly, his hand gently brushing the curve of her breast as he allowed her to step back from him. 'Do you remember that day, Kate?'

Did she? Of course she did. They had had nowhere to go where they could be alone other than the lonely clifftops, free of walkers in that cold summer, and it had been there, in a protected hollow where the wind seemed not to reach them, that Joss had lain her down and gently and tenderly shown her the mystery of her own body. He hadn't rushed her, caressing her breasts with his hands, his eyes glowing with a response that was like heady wine to her when she saw how she reacted to his touch. She had literally trembled like an aspen in his arms at the shock of discovering how she felt when he touched her like that. He had soothed her with gentle kisses and soft words of love, and then later, when she was calmer, he had touched her again, and more... She shivered, remembering how he had first removed her sweater and then had unfastened her woollen blouse.

The sensation of his hands on her bare breasts for the first time had made her cry out with pleasure. He had unfastened his own shirt and pulled her into the warmth of his body.

It had been during that afternoon, when she was half delirious with pleasure and love, that she had experienced for the first time the almost unbearable pleasure of his mouth tugging on her taut nipples.

A wave of heat broke over her. She couldn't move...speak...say or do anything as her body relived just how she had felt.

'Kate...'

She heard the anxiety in Joss's voice, as though it came from a long way away. She saw his head lift as he reached out to touch her arm, concern furrowing his forehead. Instinctively she moved back, not wanting any physical contact between them, but her movements were jerky and uncoordinated, and instead of avoiding his touch completely she caused his hand to brush the swollen peak of her breast.

'Kate.'

'Sophy and John will be here soon... Shall I make some coffee? They'll want a drink. It will help to break the ice...'

She was gabbling inanities, but she didn't care.
She didn't care about anything other than putting
a safe distance between them. If Joss said anything
about her reaction to him she would die of
embarrassment.

She willed him not to speak, but, if somewhere
inside she was still a girl of sixteen, he was no longer
a boy of twenty-one. Ignoring the imploring appeal
darkening her eyes, he asked quietly, 'What's
wrong? You're not embarrassed about this, are
you?'

As he asked the question his hand brushed lightly
over her pulsing breast, his eyes holding her own.

Oh, what was he trying to do to her? He must
know she was embarrassed.

She gave him an agonised look, her skin uncomfortably hot and tight.

'You shouldn't be,' he continued easily. 'I consider it a very great compliment. It is, after all, a
perfectly natural thing,' he told her, still watching
her, 'and a completely instinctive one. Something
over which we have virtually no control. I was just
as aroused as you.'

Kate made an inarticulate sound in her throat.
She wasn't used to conversations of this intimacy.
It was bad enough that Joss had realised what had
happened to her, but to talk about it... If he had
any tact at all he could have pretended he hadn't
noticed, just as she'd pretended she hadn't noticed
his arousal.

'As a matter of fact, I still am,' he added ruefully, a smile curving the corners of his mouth, as
though he was inviting her to share a moment of

intimate amusement. 'And quite honestly there's nothing I'd like more right now than to take you to bed and discover if your breasts are still as beautiful as they were when...'

It had gone on long enough. Too long. She wasn't an adolescent, constrained by convention and rules any more; she was an adult.

Taking a deep breath, Kate told him shortly, 'Well, they're not. That was over twenty years ago, Joss. Since then I've had a child and...'

She wasn't prepared for the way his whole face darkened as hot colour stormed it.

'*My* child,' he reminded her rawly. 'Oh, Kate...'

The doorbell rang, causing them both to tense.

'That will be Sophy and John,' Kate said huskily, smoothing her damp palms surreptitiously on her skirt as she fought to dismiss the sensations he had conjured up inside her. 'I... You'd better let them in.'

'I still don't think I can believe it.' Joss shook his head tiredly and dropped down into a chair. 'What do you honestly think, Kate? You know her—I don't. She seemed to want to get to know me.'

'She did,' Kate assured him quietly.

Sophy and John had only just gone, and it was ten o'clock at night. In the end, rather than go out for a meal as Sophy and John had planned, leaving Joss alone, when Kate realised that father and daughter were completely absorbed in one another, in exchanging facts and information about their separate lives, she had slipped into the kitchen and prepared a light meal of salad and omelettes, sensing that it would be wrong to risk damaging the rapport that was already building between Joss and Sophy by reminding them that it was well into the evening and that none of them had eaten.

John, who had followed her into the kitchen, had helped her. Kate had already liked Sophy's husband, but now she discovered that she was also going to love him as he told her quietly, 'You're being wonderful about this. I don't know if I could have been so generous in your shoes...'

'It's hard not to feel a little jealous,' Kate admitted openly, 'but they have a right to know and love one another. I'm feeling partly to blame for the fact that I allowed myself to be deceived about him. Perhaps if I'd tried harder to contact him...'

'You mustn't feel guilty,' John had told her firmly. 'And don't start thinking that Sophy blames you in any way. Only today on the way here she said that, if and when we have children, if she could be half the mother you were to her she'd be satisfied.'

'A mother, yes... but she had no father.'

'She had a marvellous grandfather,' John reminded her briskly, 'and she's one of the most secure, well-adjusted people I've ever met. No hangups at all. She also has the wisdom not to judge people too harshly or too quickly... to always look for the good in the blackest of souls; and I know she's learned that from you.'

It had brought a brief sting of tears to Kate's eyes, when, as they left, Sophy after a moment's hesitation had hugged and kissed Joss with a warmth that had plainly brought him dangerously close to tears.

Then she had taken hold of Kate's arm, and whisked her out into the corridor to say lovingly, 'Ma, you're wonderful. I love you heaps and heaps, and I can't thank you enough for letting this happen.'

'I doubt I could have stopped it,' Kate had responded wryly, and to her surprise Sophy had shaken her head.

'Yes, you could. Joss...Dad told me that if you'd refused to give him permission to do so he wouldn't have approached me. He felt in the circumstances that he didn't have the right. He's asked John and me to spend a weekend with him at his country house. I've accepted. He's going to invite you as well. You will go, won't you, Ma? I need you to be there...'

Her plea, so similar to Joss's earlier, weakened her defences, and she found that she was nodding before she had even thought properly about it.

Now Sophy and John had gone, Sophy almost floating on a cloud of euphoric delight—and why not? It wasn't every day that a girl found her father...and, moreover, found a father who was like Joss.

Kate herself felt tired and drained, but Joss was plainly exhausted. She offered to make some supper for him, but he shook his head. 'I don't think I'm capable of eating,' he told her wryly. 'I think that was the second most traumatic event in my life.'

She wanted to ask him what the first had been, suspecting that it was probably his divorce, but to her surprise he added softly, 'And in case you're wondering, the first was losing you.' He reached out for her hand, clasping it between his own.

His eyes were closed, his body lean and relaxed. Dressed casually as he was today, in many ways he seemed no different than he had done at twenty-one; his chest was broader, his face and body tougher, but apart from that . . .

'Come here, Kate,' he said roughly, without opening his eyes, the grip of his hands on hers suddenly tensing as she tried to pull away.

'Joss,' she protested, 'I . . .'

'I just want to hold you,' he told her emotionally. 'I just need to feel *close* to someone, Kate. Today highlighted for me how empty my life is . . . if I needed it highlighting.'

It was the bitterness in the words that undermined her; that, and the pain she could sense he was trying to control.

Seeing Sophy, being with her, could only have reinforced all that he had missed during the years she was growing up. That was not her fault, but it was not Joss's either, and so she went to him, and allowed him to pull her down into his arms so that she was practically lying full-length against him as he stretched out his legs to support her and wrapped his arms around her, tucking her head into his shoulder.

'It feels so good to hold you like this, Kate.'

It felt good to her, too . . . Too good. Every time she breathed she was conscious of the sheer male allure of him, the scent and heat of him, the knowledge that his flesh and hers had once been joined to produce the miracle of a child. That knowledge was a very erotic and dangerous stimulant to a body that was already over-stimulated, Kate acknowledged uncomfortably.

She couldn't move without touching Joss; she was already virtually pressed to him from shoulder to thigh, but one arm was stuck uncomfortably beneath her, and the other... The other seemed to have nowhere to go that didn't involve physical contact with one part or another of him.

Joss seemed oblivious to her tension. His eyes were closed, and his breathing had become slow and even, almost as though he was asleep.

Asleep... Cautiously Kate raised her head and looked at him.

He *was* asleep.

A tiny curl of chagrin-cum-amusement fluttered through her stomach. There she was, terrified of betraying how she felt about him, and all the time he was asleep. Chagrin and amusement battled it out and amusement won. Smiling to herself, she started to pull away from him, but his arms were locked round her and refused to release her.

As she frowned and looked into his sleeping face, he muttered her name and tightened his hold on her. There was obviously no way she was going to escape without waking him, and he looked so peaceful that she simply didn't have the heart.

Cautiously removing her numb arm, Kate positioned herself so that she was more comfortable, curling her arms around Joss as his were curled around her. After all, what did it matter what she did when he was asleep?

It seemed to matter a great deal. Her body responded to the stimulation of being close to his in a way that made her grind her teeth and question her own sanity, but she was tired too, and the steady rise and fall of Joss's chest had a soporific effect on her.

She felt her eyes close as though her eyelids were too heavy to stay open.

She woke up in the cool, clear light of the summer dawn shining through the uncurtained window, blinking and stretching, or at least *trying* to and then finding that she couldn't because she was still wrapped in Joss's arms.

Joss . . . She tried to ease away from him, but his arms tightened until she stopped moving, and then he nuzzled her throat sleepily, his eyes opening.

'Kate?'

His voice held surprise.

'Let me go, Joss,' she demanded. 'We both fell asleep.'

'We certainly did,' he agreed, sitting up but not releasing her. He looked at his watch.

'Four o'clock in the morning.' He gave a soft groan.

Heaven alone knew what she must look like, Kate thought acidly, ducking her head instinctively.

He saw the movement and eyed her gravely, and then reached out and very deliberately scooped her hair off her face and looked at her.

'Come to bed with me, Kate,' he suggested softly.

Perhaps she ought not to have been stunned, but she was. All right, she had aroused him to desire, but she hadn't thought that that desire had anything personal in it.

She looked wildly away from him, colour fluctuating under her skin. This was no light-hearted teasing. The question had been put seriously to her, and she prayed no one bar herself would ever know just how tempted she was to say yes.

But that wasn't the way she lived. She couldn't make love with Joss now and then casually put him out of her mind.

'Come to bed with me,' he repeated against her ear, sending fine shivers of sensation racing over her skin. 'I want you, Kate...'

'No. You don't,' she told him flatly, pushing away from him. 'Not really. You think you do because... because of the emotional trauma of everything that's happened. It wouldn't be sensible. We'd both regret it...'

She didn't want to look at him, but she had to.

'Would we?' he asked her bleakly, and then added, 'Perhaps you're right. Sensible Kate. The Kate I knew wasn't sensible at all, was she?'

'No,' Kate agreed shortly, as she pulled away from him and was set free. 'And look what happened to her...'

It was an unfair gibe, but it had hurt that he should call her sensible in such a derisive way, reminding her of all the things she had striven to remember these last few weeks. Reminding her that she was a woman and not a girl... that she had gone beyond the age where she could carelessly make love for no better reason than that she desired to.

And there was another complication. One that she hesitated to mention to Joss, which was surely idiotic in the circumstances. She used no method of birth control, never having had the necessity.

It was still possible for her to conceive...and not just possible at this particular time of the month but probable, she acknowledged, especially given her past record.

She tried to imagine telling Sophy that she was having Joss's child, and was stunned by the sudden spasmodic sensation inside her, as though a wanton, intimate part of her actually wanted to conceive that child.

The sensation was unfamiliar to her. At sixteen she had not really thought beyond the pleasure of the moment, and certainly not as far as actually wanting to conceive a child.

There was a silence, and then Joss said abruptly, 'I don't know about you, but it hardly seems worth while going to sleep now. I'm a member of a health club a short walk from here. I think a swim and an hour in the gym is what's called for right now. Fancy coming with me?'

Kate shook her head.

'No...I might as well pack and catch an earlier train home,' she told him.

His expression hardened.

'If that's what you want to do...'

No, it wasn't what she wanted to do at all. What she wanted to do was to hold out her arms to him...to make love with him...to be *with* him because she loved him, and, knowing that, she couldn't allow herself to take the risk of burdening him with feelings and responsibilities that he couldn't possibly want.

'I think it would be best,' she told him carefully.

'Best ... safest ... How cautious you've become, Kate.'

'I've had to be,' she retorted, stung by the hardness in his words.

She put her hand to her temple, realising that they were on the verge of a quarrel.

'Perhaps you're right,' Joss said quietly. 'Perhaps we do need to distance ourselves from one another a little ... But you will join Sophy and John the weekend after next when they come down to my place, won't you?'

'Sophy wants me to,' she said uncertainly. 'But if you'd rather I didn't ...'

'Why do you always assume *I* don't want your company, Kate?'

She turned her face away from him.

'A legacy of the past, I suppose,' he sighed, answering his own question. 'Well, we both carry those burdens. I'd like you to be there. It's going to take quite a while for Sophy and me to be completely at ease with one another. She's very protective of you, you know, and even now that she knows the truth I suspect that, in her eyes, I'll always be the man who uncaringly made a girl of sixteen pregnant.'

Kate bit her lip, hearing the weary resignation in his voice.

'You didn't know,' she said painfully. 'You thought that I was older and ...'

'Protected. Yes . . . I know, but with hindsight I ought to have guessed the truth; you were so innocent, so inexperienced——' He broke off, shaking his head and reverting to his earlier question.

'You will be there then, the weekend after next?'

'If Lucy can stand in for me again. You'll have to give me the address . . . I'll probably drive down.'

'No. I'll come and collect you.'

'There's no need for that. I can quite easily find my own way.'

'Yes, I expect you can. But I've had a lifetime of being in a position of not being able or allowed to do things for those close to me, Kate, so humour me a little, will you? Let me . . . cherish you a little now, for all the times I wasn't there to do so.'

Cherish her? A ripple of emotion ran through her and she wondered if he had chosen the words deliberately or had just happened on it by accident. And why cherish *her*? It should be Sophy he was cherishing. Unless . . . unless he hoped to impress Sophy by his concern for her. But that seemed so out of character. She had been struck now, as she had been in the past, by his complete honesty and openness in everything he said and did. He watched her and then said softly, 'Well, if you won't sleep with me, and you won't come to the gym with me, will you at least stay and have breakfast with me?'

Kate gave him an amused smile, her tension gone.

'Only if you promise that I don't have to eat it until after seven o'clock.'

'I'll tell you what, since we missed out on afternoon tea at the Ritz, how about having brunch at the Inn on the Park?' he suggested.

She would be safer there among other people than here alone with him, and so she nodded, and then escaped to her bedroom before he could drag any more dangerous promises from her.

CHAPTER NINE

THE PHONE was ringing as Kate unlocked the front door. She put down her bag and ran to pick it up. A feather of disappointment tingled down her spine when she discovered it was Sophy.

Who had she expected it to be? Joss? Guiltily she remembered the warm kiss he had given her when he'd left her. He had insisted on escorting her to the station and then waiting until the train left.

It had left a warm, tremulous feeling inside her, that brief meeting of lips just before the train pulled out.

Careful, she warned herself. Careful, Kate. Both of you are caught up in an emotional backlash that will very quickly fizzle out. On Joss's side, at least.

'You're back, then,' Sophy announced. 'I rang Joss's flat and he said you'd left. I don't know if I'm ever going to be able to call him "Dad"!' she mused, and then added breathlessly, 'Oh, Ma, it's all happened so fast . . . I can hardly take it all in. And you must be feeling the same. Discovering, after all these years, that he did love you. He could hardly take his eyes off you on Saturday.'

'Don't be ridiculous,' Kate objected firmly.

She could almost see Sophy's thought processes ticking away and adding up, and she didn't like the sums her daughter was making.

'This is life, Sophy,' she warned her. 'Not a novel. Don't start thinking that Joss and I mean anything more to one another than...'

'Than any other two people who've had a child together?' Sophy suggested softly. And then apologised. 'I'm sorry, Ma. It's just... well, he seems so lonely, despite his success and everything. And he did ask you to stay with him.'

'Because he couldn't get me into a hotel,' Kate told her firmly.

'And so you don't feel anything for him... not even the slightest, teeniest twinge?'

Kate opened her mouth to fib and then changed her mind.

'Of course I do,' she admitted honestly. 'But, Sophy, remember this is a very emotional time for all of us. It wouldn't be sensible or fair for any of us to take things that are said or which happen now too seriously. Later, when we're all able to distance ourselves a little... when we're not acting out of character in the emotional heat of the moment...'

Although she was talking to Sophy, she was trying to rationalise to herself Joss's desire for her.

It wasn't a desire born of love, but a desire born of shock, pain, remorse and a hundred other emotions, none of which had anything to do with the fierce, searing recognition *she* had experienced the moment she had looked at him and had known that nothing had changed and that she still loved him.

His feelings weren't like that. They couldn't be. If he did fall in love again, it would be with someone younger, like Lucille; someone young and beautiful... not like her.

'Well, you are going to be there the weekend after next, aren't you?' Sophy asked.

'If you're sure you want me to be.'

'Yes. Yes, I do. It's wonderful, of course, but it still seems a little strange. I've got to put aside the image I've always had of my father and try to put Joss in his place.'

They talked for a few more minutes and, having satisfied herself that her daughter was coping very well with the trauma of discovering that Joss was her father, Kate replaced the receiver.

She ought to ring Lucy and find out how she had coped over the weekend, but she felt exhausted. Another reminder that she was not sixteen any more.

She sank down into a chair, and groaned as she looked through the kitchen window and realised that the lawn needed mowing. How on earth had it managed to grow so much in such a short space of time? Sophy was always telling her that she should get someone in to do the gardens, but she enjoyed doing it herself... normally.

Yes, hard work was what she needed, she told herself briskly. It would stop her mooning around like a silly girl, daydreaming impossible day-dreams, which all featured Joss.

As though she had made a wish, Kate had one of the busiest fortnights she had ever experienced.

For a start there was a mild epidemic of a stomach virus which claimed Lucy as one of its victims, necessitating Kate's not only shouldering her partner's share of the work, but also stepping in to take and collect Lucy's children from school, leaving their father to attend to his clients.

A little to her amusement, Kate discovered that she quite enjoyed the return to being the 'mother' of young children. It came as a surprise to discover how many older mothers there were among the women waiting to collect their offspring, some of them very obviously her own age and older.

It must be the new fashion for women establishing their careers before taking time off to have their families, Kate reflected tiredly on Thursday evening as she finished unpacking the groceries she had bought earlier from the supermarket.

They had only had two bookings for the weekend, and, realising that Lucy wasn't going to be well enough to cope with them, Kate had cancelled them. Luckily both parties had been very understanding, and neither booking had been for a major event.

Joss was due to come and collect her tomorrow afternoon. Sophy was ringing this evening to confirm all the arrangements.

At last! Kate sat back on her heels as the last of her shopping was disposed of. The phone rang as though on cue, and she went to answer it.

As she had hoped, it was Sophy, bubbling over with enthusiasm and happiness.

'You'll never guess what,' Sophy announced once she had confirmed everything. 'Do you remember the woman Joss brought to the wedding? His secretary? Well, he's sacked her!'

'Sacked her?'

'Mm, John told me.'

Joss had sacked Lucille! That was no real reason for her heart to suddenly start thudding as though she had run a race, and yet later, when she was in bed, she found that she was as excited as a child at the thought of Christmas, unable to sleep because she knew that tomorrow she'd see him . . . be with him . . . The weekend stretched out ahead of her, dazzling her with its promise . . . dangerously alluring.

She was awake early, still filled with that dangerous anticipation.

By ten o'clock her small case was packed, and she was virtually ready. Joss hadn't said what time he would arrive, just that it would be early in the afternoon.

She intended to travel in a plain cream pleated skirt with a matching cotton knit sweater . . . a new outfit she had bought on impulse. One of several new outfits she had bought on impulse, she was ashamed to admit.

She had washed her hair and put on her make-up; the house was clean and tidy; she had nothing to do but sit and wait for Joss.

Ridiculous, she told herself, and if she wanted something to do there was always the garden. The lawn badly needed mowing . . . again.

Sighing faintly, she went upstairs and changed into a pair of faded shorts and a brief top. It was hot outside, and mowing the lawn would make her even hotter, as she knew from experience.

It did . . . less than half-way through she had to stop and go inside to get a cool drink and to tie her hair back off her face, with a piece of ribbon she managed to find in the kitchen drawer.

Thank goodness there was no one to see her, she reflected, grimacing at her slim, bare legs, her feet in grubby trainers, her shorts a faded, worn pair she had had for years, and her top a once-pristine white strappy affair, which now had the odd grass stain.

The mower was an old one, petrol-driven and inclined to be temperamental. It had belonged to her father, and Kate kept it because basically she was too lazy to replace it.

She had virtually finished, and was just going down the final strip, her back to the house, when Joss appeared.

She hadn't heard him arrive, and he stood and waited for her to turn round, watching her, a faint smile of amusement curling his mouth as he took in her untidy ponytail and bare legs.

Kate turned round, and then stopped dead.

Oh, no . . . it couldn't be. It wasn't even twelve yet. She wanted to run and hide, and yet she couldn't move, her feet almost glued to the spot where she stood as Joss strolled casually over the lawn towards her.

He was wearing an immaculately crisp white cotton shirt and a pair of well-fitting, and *clean*, denims.

She felt horribly grubby and hot, uncomfortably conscious of her appalling appearance . . . of the sweat trickling down the back of her neck . . . of the way her thin cotton top was clinging to her body... of the bareness of her legs and the inelegance of her untidy hair.

'You look hot,' Joss commented as he reached her, his smile doing nothing to calm her agitation.

'I am,' she said shortly, and then added accusingly, 'You're early.'

'Yes. It's such a lovely day, I thought we might stop on the way back and have lunch somewhere.'

'There's no need. Anyway, I would have thought you'd have wanted to get back as quickly as possible so that you can spend as much time as you can with Sophy.'

Her accusatory tone made him frown.

'An excellent idea,' he agreed urbanely, 'but Sophy and John aren't arriving until later on tonight, after they've both finished work.'

It was on the tip of her tongue to tell him that in that case he had had no need to pick her up so early, but she realised in time that she was behaving churlishly and perhaps betrayingly, and so she gave him a forced smile and said ruefully, 'Well, as you can see, I wasn't expecting you. I'd better go in and get changed.'

Her face felt hot from the sun and the exertion, and she hated the contrast she must make to Joss's cool and physically compelling presence. It was one thing to accept that he couldn't feel about her the way she did about him; it was quite another to have to confront him looking the way she did right now... far from at her best.

He leaned forward, reaching out to touch her, and immediately she flinched, moving back.

'What's wrong?' He was frowning at her, his earlier smile gone.

What was wrong? How like a man. Surely he could *see* what was wrong? Here she was with her hair tied up in that idiotic ponytail, with wisps of it clinging to her hot, sticky face...wearing grubby clothes...clothes, moreover, that no sensible woman of her age would ever wear in front of a man she wanted to admire her. At sixteen she just...just might have been able to get away with such an outfit, but more than twenty years on...

'I don't want you to touch me,' she said defensively, and then, as his frown deepened, she felt forced to add, 'I'm filthy—hot and...' She couldn't bring herself to say the word 'sweaty', even if it was the only one that was appropriate.

'What's wrong, Kate?' he asked her quietly. 'The Kate *I* remember wouldn't have minded being seen looking the way you look right now.'

It was the gentleness in his voice that she couldn't stand. It made her feel far too vulnerable. She reacted to it immediately and angrily.

'That was over twenty years ago.'

'And that's supposed to make a difference? Not to me,' he told her, shaking his head.

She didn't want to listen to this. She couldn't afford to listen. She turned away from him abruptly, too abruptly, walking straight into the mower, and jarring her hipbone so painfully that she stumbled.

It was Joss who caught her, one arm supporting her back, his hand splayed across the bare flesh between her top and her shorts, the other resting on her throbbing hip, massaging the bruised flesh.

Heat sprang from her pores as though her body was in flames. She wrenched back from him, but he wouldn't let her go.

'Joss, let me go,' she protested. 'I'm dirty and . . . and . . . stick . . .'

'Sweaty,' he said calmly for her, reaching up, and catching a bead of sweat that rolled down her neck.

Her face flamed in an agony of embarrassment, and then, at the way he was looking at her, the garden swayed dizzily around her, so dizzily that she had to clutch his forearms for support.

He couldn't really mean what she could see in his eyes . . . He couldn't really desire her, not like this.

She must have said the words out loud without knowing it, because he replied thickly, 'Just like this. You're a woman, not a mechanical doll, Kate, and the scent and heat of you is driving me out of my mind. Feel,' he demanded rawly, taking her hand and placing it against his body before she could stop him.

The whole universe stood still. Kate couldn't have moved, no matter who or what commanded it. Every nerve-ending in her body was concentrated on the fierce, aroused pulse of him.

She made a soft, inarticulate sound in her throat, a tiny mewling cry of panic blended with pleasure. She felt his mouth moving against her throat, tasting its moist saltiness. She shivered, and the light pressure of his mouth became the harder, more demanding bite of his teeth.

Her top had tiny buttons down the front which she never unfastened, but they were unfastened now and Joss's hand was pushing away the fabric, not just so that he could touch her, but so that he could look at her as well, she realised.

It was too late now to wish she had worn a bra...to wish that they were not standing in the cruel sunlight of the garden where it was plain for him to see that her breasts, which at not quite sixteen had been as round and hard as apples, were now fuller, softer; too womanly really for her to go without the support of a bra, but her top was brief and she had been alone in the garden...or so she had thought.

She tensed and tried to pull away, to hide herself, but he wouldn't let her, turning her so that her hip pushed against him and one arm imprisoned her, one hand holding her arm at her side while his other hand pushed away the open sides of her top.

The tension was unbearable. She knew he was looking at her, and knowing what he was seeing made her clench her hands and cry out, 'Please don't...don't look at me.'

'Why not? You're beautiful.'

'No!' she cried rawly, her voice tormented.

'Yes,' Joss told her fiercely. 'More so now than you were before!' And then he asked her raggedly, as though unable to stop himself, 'Sophy...when she was a baby, did you feed her yourself?'

Colour invaded his cheekbones as she looked at him. Why had he asked that?

'Yes,' she told him. 'I wanted to do my best for her, and they said at the hospital...'

The ground was shaking, she discovered suddenly, and then she realised it wasn't, that it was
Joss shuddering.

She forgot her nudity, her embarrassment and
anxiety as she clutched the front of his shirt and
begged worriedly, 'Joss, what's wrong? What's
wrong?'

'What's   wrong?   Everything...everything's
wrong. All the things you and I never shared which
we *should* have shared... Would you have another
child?' he asked her suddenly.

Another child. Strangely, the thought wasn't as
alien or shocking as it should have been.

'If I were married,' she said slowly. 'If I were in
a committed, stable relationship with someone who
loved me...then yes, I think I would. But since
that's not likely to happen...'

Her face flamed as she realised that she was
standing in the half-circle of his arm with her breasts
completely exposed and that she wasn't making the
slightest attempt to conceal them, but as she moved
Joss moved too, and he was faster than her, his
hand sliding slowly over her tender skin, his palm
scraping the delicate nipple, which immediately
hardened and pulsed.

'I must go and have a shower...get changed...'

'Not yet,' he whispered in a thick, strained voice.
'Not yet, Kate. Let me hold you just for a moment.'

She wanted to protest. She knew she *ought* to
protest, but for some reason she didn't...couldn't.
All she could do was simply cling to him while his
hands stroked over and over her sensitive skin,
arousing her to the point where she was trembling

with the force of the sensations building up inside her.

She wanted him to kiss her, ached for him to do so, and yet was terrified that if he did...*once* he did, she wouldn't be able to stop herself from begging him to make love to her.

When he released her she felt bereft...empty and aching inside.

'If I don't stop now, I won't be able to.'

The words reached her from a distance and she clung to them, trying to remind herself that this was real...that *Joss* was real. She lifted her head and looked at him, aching to ask him why he was doing this to her, and yet unable to do so. Not really wanting to hear the answer, for there could be so many complex reasons...none of them having anything to do with love.

'I think I'd better wait out here for you,' he told her grimly. 'It will be safer—for both of us.'

They stopped for lunch, just north of the Cotswolds, in a small, sleepy village of ancient stone houses, and it was just gone seven o'clock when Joss told Kate that they were approaching the outskirts of his home.

'The village is only small, and thankfully too far from London for commuters. I only found it by chance. The house is tucked away down a lane behind the church. It was the original rectory. The Victorians built a new one.'

The lane was overgrown with summer hedgerows and wild flowers. Kate wound down the car window to breathe in the rich smell of growing things. A couple of rabbits were playing on the rutted road ahead of them, quickly disappearing when they heard the car.

'Once I move here permanently I think I'll get a dog,' Joss told her, as they reached the end of the lane and he turned in through an open gateway without any gates. 'You like dogs, don't you, Kate?'

'Yes,' she agreed, adding drily, 'and so does Sophy.'

He shot her an enigmatic look. 'Here we are,' he announced.

The house was older and larger than she had imagined, set in a garden so wild and overgrown it was impossible to imagine what it had once been.

'It was empty for a couple of years before I bought it. Come on. It's a bit better inside than it looks.'

It was. Inside the Elizabethan façade, work had already started on repairs and renovations.

'I had all the plumbing and wiring stripped out and replaced,' Joss told her, as they walked into a panelled hallway, 'and the bathrooms and kitchen gutted and replaced—but that's about as far as I've got. One of the sitting-rooms is fairly habitable. I'll show you.'

It was, just, Kate agreed, grimacing at the dull parquet floor and uninspired décor, and yet it had the potential to be a lovely room. It overlooked a walled garden to the side of the house, which was just as wild as the main one, and even now in the early evening the garden was bathed in warmth and sunlight.

'How many rooms are there?' Kate asked curiously.

'Seven bedrooms, four bathrooms; and downstairs, a drawing-room, dining-room, study, this room and a large kitchen. I'll show you round in a second. I'd better just check the answering machine first, if you don't mind.'

'Perhaps I could make us a drink,' Kate suggested, not wanting to be in the way.

'Mm. You'll find everything in the kitchen. Just help yourself.'

The kitchen had been fitted with natural oak units; a gleaming scarlet Aga stood in an alcove against soft reddish-pink bricks. The floor had been covered in muted terracotta tiles, and Kate fell in love with it instantly. She deliberately took her time, carrying through a tray of tea only when she judged that Joss had had sufficient time to play back his messages.

When she went into the sitting-room he was standing with his back to the window, frowning as he drummed his fingers against the back of a chair.

'Something wrong?' she asked him.

'Yes, I'm afraid so. Sophy and John won't be able to make it.'

He saw her expression and said quickly, 'No, nothing like that. They're both fine, but John's boss has asked them to help him entertain some American clients tomorrow evening.' He spread his hands. 'Naturally there was no way they could get out of it. He tried to reach me at the office, but I'd already left to pick you up.'

Kate's body slumped at the thought of the long drive back. Summoning a bright smile, she said, 'It's just as well I haven't unpacked isn't it? I suppose if we don't stop to eat, I could be back...'

'Potentially,' Joss agreed drily, and then added, 'But it isn't essential that you get back tonight, is it?' He flexed his shoulders as he spoke, as though they ached from driving.

She was being selfish, Kate recognised. Another long drive was probably the last thing Joss felt like.

'No, not really,' she agreed.

'Then let's sit down and drink this tea and plan how we're going to spend the weekend,' Joss suggested easily.

'The *weekend*? But Joss, I can't stay here now.'

'Why not?'

She looked at him, nonplussed.

'Well...no reason...but you can't *want* me to. I mean, the whole idea of my being here was because Sophy and John were going to be here.'

'And now they're not going to be here, but you are.' He gave her a thoughtful look and then said, straight-faced, 'We could always make a start on the garden. With your expertise with a mower...'

Kate laughed.

'A *mower*? What you need is a combine harvester,' she mocked. 'How on earth did the garden get in such a state?'

'I've no idea,' Joss told her drolly. 'I think it's something called Nature. I've got a firm coming in in the autumn to start clearing it.'

'It's a wonderful project,' Kate murmured half wistfully. 'What will you do? Restore it to its original Tudor design?'

'I'd like to... perhaps you could help me. Gardening isn't my forte.'

Flattered and pleased, Kate made a non-committal response. She mustn't allow herself to get too involved... too close.

Joss glanced at his watch.

'I've booked a table for us at a restaurant a couple of miles away. I said we'd be there about half-past eight.'

'We could have eaten here,' Kate protested.

'Not unless all we have to eat is cold meat and salad,' Joss told her forthrightly. 'I'm too tired to start cooking, and I'm damn sure you feel the same way.'

She did, but she was surprised that he should have realised it and made provision for it. She wasn't used to people doing things for her... considering her... caring for her, she recognised on a wistful pang of envy for the woman who might one day share Joss's life. He combined the best of both worlds: he had strength without force; tenderness without weakness; maleness without aggression.

'I'll get my case in from the car and get changed.'

'I'll bring it in for you,' he told her, pausing as he got up to add softly, 'If you've got anything silky with you, Kate, wear it for me, will you?'

Silky... the only thing she had that fitted that description was a cream silk shirt. And *wear* it for him. A tiny shiver convulsed her. Why?

*   *   *

It didn't take her long to change and she did wear the silk shirt, despite the fact that half of her hadn't really wanted to do.

Joss was waiting for her at the bottom of the stairs. He looked up as she walked towards him and a delicious tingle of pleasure raced through her as he watched her.

'Nice,' he told her as she reached the bottom of the stairs, and his hand brushed lightly against her breast, so lightly that she might almost have imagined it.

'But it would be even nicer if you weren't wearing this,' he added as his fingertip traced the strap of her bra. 'Take it off, Kate.'

Take it off? She stared at him.

'I can't . . .' she told him quickly. 'I can't go out like that.'

'Yes, you can,' he argued, and before she could stop him his fingers were deftly unfastening the buttons of her shirt and reaching behind her for the snap fastening of her bra.

Another moment and she'd be as exposed to him as she had been this afternoon, she realised, panicking, pushing him away quickly, saying huskily, 'All right, all right. But I'll do it myself . . .'

'Are you sure you don't want me to help?' he teased as he stepped back from her, and as she escaped to her room to remove the scrap of underwear and hurriedly refasten her shirt Kate wondered what on earth was happening to her. This was so at odds with her normal staid, cautious approach to life. She stopped and frowned wistfully, wondering if over the years she had become so terrified of stepping out of the mould she had made for herself that she had forgotten the value of occasionally living spontaneously, and perhaps even a little dangerously.

Well, if so, she was certainly doing so, she acknowledged wryly as she gave herself a last half-worried look at her reflection.

It was true that her silk shirt was tailored and modest enough to prevent the casual observer being aware that she wore nothing beneath it, but Joss wasn't a casual observer. And why had he made such an extraordinary request in the first place?

She paused, torn between an eager longing to walk through the door he seemed to be holding open for her, inviting her into a new and unfamiliar world, and an urge to firmly turn her back on that invitation.

It was impossible to pretend to herself any longer. Joss quite plainly wanted them to become lovers, but why, and for how long?

She suspected she knew the truth, and while had the circumstances been different, had she not still loved him, she could have merely basked in the flattery of knowing that he desired her…could even perhaps have quite easily and pleasurably made love with him in the knowledge that in doing so she was taking a light-hearted journey into nostalgia, knowing that she *did* love him made it impossible for her to respond to his flattery without risking betraying how she felt.

As for how long his desire might last… She was pretty sure that, like his nostalgia, it would disappear once she became a concrete reality in his life.

As she hesitated in the large, rather bare bedroom Joss had given her, she knew she had two choices in front of her. The most sensible thing she could do now was to tell Joss firmly and calmly that he was wasting his time and that she had no intention of allowing them to become lovers. For her own self-protection that was her safest course, but when she heard him demand from the bottom of the stairs, 'Kate? Is anything wrong?' she knew that she wasn't going to be wise or sensible.

CHAPTER TEN

'Mm...that was heaven,' Kate said appreciatively as she scooped up the last mouthful of soufflé.

The restaurant had provided them with a meal that made her glad that Joss had insisted on them eating out. Mouthwateringly luscious melon filled with crushed, flavoured crystals of ice; salmon in the lightest, most tempting of delicately flavoured sauces; tiny new potatoes, and vegetables which her palate recognised as locally grown, followed by the most delicious soufflé.

'You always did have a sweet tooth,' Joss said drily. He had opted for cheese and biscuits.

Defensively Kate pushed aside her empty dish and said crossly, 'Yes, I know at my age I ought to have developed more sophisticated tastes, but I——'

The hand that reached across the table to grip her own made her tense with surprise. Joss shook her wrist reprovingly.

'Kate, I am tired of hearing you mentioning your age. You are a very beautiful and desirable woman, who in my eyes at least has reached the perfect age.'

Flushing a little, Kate pulled her hand away. All through the meal their conversation had been general and absorbing, but without any hint of sexual innuendo, and she had allowed her defences to fall.

'You don't believe me, do you?' Joss said flatly, watching the shadows cross her face.

'It's only natural that a man should be more attracted to a girl in her twenties than a woman in...'

'Her mid-thirties. Ridiculous,' Joss told her roundly. 'Sure there are men...men of my own age and older, who because of their own insecurities and immaturity feel the need to boost their own egos by becoming some kind of Svengali-cum-father-figure to a much younger woman, but I'd feel insulted to be classed with them, Kate. I consider myself far too well-adjusted to need that kind of bolster. The plain fact is that youth, while attractive in its own way, is often shallow and self-centred...which is as it should be. Every age has its own gifts, and to imply that I, at damn near forty-three, would prefer the company of the girl you were to the woman you are is as ridiculous as suggesting that you would find the company of the boy I was at twenty-one more stimulating than the man I am...or perhaps you *would*?'

Kate shook her head immediately, flushing.

'Exactly,' Joss told her wryly.

There was a small silence, while Kate hunted desperately for something to say.

'Sophy told me that Lucille isn't working for you any longer,' she said at last.

Joss frowned. 'No, that's right.' He lifted his head and looked directly at her. 'I thought it best in the circumstances, for her sake. While we had an excellent business relationship, I became aware recently that she felt a certain degree of...personal attachment to me, which, since I could not return it, meant that for her own sake it was best that she left my employ.'

As she listened to him, Kate shivered a little. This was the other side of him, logical and ruthless almost. When he no longer desired her, was that how he would dismiss her from his life?

'We were never lovers, Kate.' He said it calmly, almost so quietly that she didn't hear him.

'You've said that before.'

'And you don't believe me.'

'I do believe you, but I'm not really sure why you felt it necessary to tell me,' she said incautiously.

There, it was out in the open between them. She had learned over the years not to avoid facing difficult or intimidating situations. Joss had made it clear that he desired her; now she was giving him the opportunity to quantify that desire, to tell her openly that he wanted them to be lovers.

He gave her a lightning, almost surprised glance, and then said quietly, 'Kind Kate. And that's another way in which we've changed. Then there was no need for explanations or reasons.' He reached out across the table and took her left hand in his. 'Then it was simply enough to look and touch and know...' There was a brief, tense silence and then he said huskily, 'Kate, I'd like you to marry me.'

It was the last thing she'd been expecting. Her mouth fell open and she gaped at him.

As he perceived her shock, he frowned. 'I'm sorry... but I thought you'd guessed.'

'I thought you wanted us to be lovers,' Kate told him, too stunned to prevaricate. 'I thought perhaps you were caught up in nostalgia for the past and that ...'

'I wanted to relive what we once shared.' The smile he gave her was faintly acid. 'You obviously don't have a very high opinion of my intelligence. I'm a very successful, very lonely man, Kate. You are the mother of my only child. These past few weeks have shown us both, I think, that we get on well together. I think that between us we could build a very worthwhile and sustaining relationship, one that will bring us both pleasure and contentment and one that will last for the rest of our lives.'

'"Grow old along with me!"' Kate quoted wryly. How idiotically wrong she had been. It wasn't as a desirable woman that he saw her at all, but rather as an insurance policy for their mutual old age.

It was idiotic to feel rebuffed and hurt that, instead of wanting her as his lover, he wanted her as his wife.

'As I remember it, that quotation goes on, "The best is yet to be,"' Joss reminded her, equally drily. 'I think that's how it could be for us, Kate. I think we could live here, you and I, and find joy and companionship in doing so. After all, we already have one very good reason for doing so. We have our daughter.'

'Sophy is grown up, married with a life of her own,' Kate protested, while inside her heart bled a little that in all the sensible, admirable reasons he had given for their marriage he had never once mentioned the word love.

'Think about it, Kate,' he urged her. 'I know I've rather sprung it on you, but to be honest I've been thinking about it since that weekend when I came to see you and I realised the truth...'

'I thought you said that you didn't want to marry again. That after your divorce...'

'I think I said I didn't want to make another mistake. Marrying you wouldn't be a mistake. I'd give you a totally free hand with the garden,' he tempted teasingly, 'and a new lawnmower...'

It was hard not to smile.

'I have a home...a career...'

'Yes, I know. I realise how much you'd be giving up, don't think I don't.'

She knew already what her answer was going to be. She couldn't marry him. No matter how eminently sensible and practical a course it might seem, she just could not do it. Better never to see him at all than to have the constant unremitting torment of living side by side with him in the calm, emotionless kind of relationship he had just described. Side by side...two people in reality going their separate ways through life...two people who merely appeared to be unified, but who in reality were not.

Before she could weaken she said quickly, 'No, I'm sorry, Joss. I can't marry you.'

She forced herself to look directly at him as she gave him her refusal.

The dimly lit room threw shadows across his face, but to her surprise she thought she saw a momentary bitter pain darkening his eyes.

Pain was the last thing she wanted to cause him, but even as she reached out to touch him he said crisply, 'Perhaps you're right.'

And she withdrew her hand, saying shakily, 'Without love, a marriage is just an empty shell.'

'Yes,' he agreed grimly, and Kate sighed, wondering if her unwise heart had actually hoped that he would deny her assertion and claim that he *did* love her. But why should he? They were not teenagers any more, and a good many women of her age would have jumped at the kind of relationship he was proposing. Why did she have to cling to such ridiculous teenage ideals of loving and being loved? Love could die; respect, companionship...these were much more enduring foundations on which to build a relationship. But she was greedy, she acknowledged helplessly; she wanted those and she wanted love as well.

Neither of them spoke on the way back to Joss's house. She would have enjoyed living here, taking up the challenge of restoring and loving the old house and its garden, she acknowledged wearily, and she could have remained independent of Joss financially even without working. Her house would have brought her in a comfortable capital sum, enough to make her feel that she was not totally dependent on her husband.

It was too late for second thoughts now, she told herself sternly, knowing that she was weakening and knowing that the cause of that weakness was sitting next to her here in the car, tormenting her senses with his presence. She only had to turn her head to see Joss's strong profile...to look at his mouth to immediately remember how it felt against her own; to look at his hands as they controlled the powerful car to remember how she felt when they stroked and caressed her flesh. Beneath her skin, blood thudded into vulnerable pulse points. She

moved restlessly in her seat, feeling the taut pull,
the drag of silk against her breasts, an urgent, un-
wanted need coiling in her stomach.

She thought of everything she was giving up,
turning her back on and she shuddered, racked with
regret.

'Cold?' Joss asked briefly, flicking on the heater.
'Soon be home.'

Home. If only it were. And it could be... if she
allowed herself to give in to temptation. Did Joss
realise how tempted she was? Did he know perhaps
how vulnerable she was to him? Odd, that he had
asked her to marry him without trying to coerce
her by using the most powerful strength he had. He
must know that physically she desired him, even if
he hadn't put two and two together and realised
anything else... and yet he hadn't touched her...

What had she expected? she derided herself.
Passionate kisses the moment they were alone in
the car... urgent pleas for her to change her mind?

She closed her eyes, willing her unruly thoughts
to subside, forcing herself to remain still and silent
until the car pulled up in front of the house.

'I think I'll go straight up,' she said quietly, once
they were inside. What was the point of prolonging
things? Joss had proposed, she had refused, and
now he was so uncommunicative that she knew he
wanted to be on his own.

'Not just yet,' he said abruptly. 'There's something I'd like you to have. I had hoped to be giving
it to you under different circumstances, but since
it was bought for you... I won't be a moment,' he
told her curtly, leaving her standing in the cool,

shadowy hall as he disappeared into the room that was eventually to be his study.

When he emerged he looked tense and weary. He handed her a small jeweller's box which so plainly could only hold a ring that she stared rigidly at it, unable to open it... unable even to move.

'Open it, Kate,' Joss told her grimly. 'I bought it over twenty years ago for you. When I went back to Cornwall after my father's death I took it with me, intending to ask you then to be my wife. When I discovered what I thought was the truth, I was tempted to throw it away, but I couldn't.'

'You've kept it all these years,' Kate murmured, dazed by what he was saying, unable to take her eyes off the small leather box.

'Sentimental of me, I know, but I couldn't bring myself to part with it. I had hoped that tonight I would have been able to place it on your finger.'

Tears rushed into her eyes, making them burn. Now, when it was too late, here was the evidence of emotion she had longed for when he had made that cool, common-sense proposal. If only he had said this then... All right, so maybe he *didn't* love her, but this ring... to have kept this ring... To have wanted all those years ago to marry her... It was only the tiniest, frailest tendril of hope, but it was enough; it might grow.

The tears were threatening to overflow. If she stayed where she was any longer, she'd disgrace herself completely. She needed time to think... to be alone. With a small, inarticulate cry, she closed her fingers round the box and fled upstairs.

Joss didn't follow her, and it was only when she had dried her eyes that she felt ready to open the box.

She did so with fingers that trembled. The ring inside was small and delicate...a young girl's ring, and she loved it instantly...loved the richness of the central sapphire which she had once told Joss was her favourite stone...loved the tiny encircling diamonds that sparkled so happily...loved the narrow, plain band of gold. She picked it up, and slid it on to her finger. It fitted perfectly. Fresh tears welled...tears of regret...of pain...of self-pity. She let them fall, needing their cleansing astringency, and then she took off the ring and put it back in its box. Such a small thing, and yet it changed everything. Tomorrow she would talk to Joss...tell him honestly and openly why she had refused him...explain to him that she loved him, and then, if with that knowledge he still wanted to marry her, she would do so.

He was right. They could build a good life together, but only if she was honest. She wouldn't burden him with her love without him knowing that it existed...and she wouldn't refuse him, knowing that the ring he had given her tonight symbolised everything she had thought absent from his proposal.

She undressed and showered, but once she was in bed she found it impossible to sleep. She was as tense as a small child alternating between anticipation and dread. She heard a distant church clock tolling mournfully. One o'clock and then two, and she was still as far away from sleep as ever.

And then, knowing that it was going to be impossible for her to sleep, she got up and pulled on her robe.

She knew which was Joss's room. The door was ajar, and a lamp was on inside. She crossed her fingers behind her back. If he was awake she would tell him. If he wasn't . . .

She pushed open the door and went in.

Joss was awake, lying propped up against his pillow, hands linked behind his head, his torso dark and tanned against the whiteness of the linen.

He turned his head as she walked in. A muscle twitched in his jaw and Kate fastened on that tiny human weakness. It gave her courage.

'Can we talk?' she asked quietly.

He eyed her gravely and then nodded, shifting to one side of the bed, and patting the space next to him.

'Come and sit down. You'll freeze if you stand there. Central heating's installed now, but it's not working yet.'

As she obeyed him, he said heavily, 'If you're worried that I'll try to pressure you through Sophy...'

Kate stopped him, reaching out to lay her fingers on his arm. His skin felt warm and firm, the dark hairs slightly abrasive to her fingertips. She felt her body responding to the stimulus of touching him and removed her hand hastily.

'It's not that.' She raised her head and looked at him. 'If it isn't too late, I'd like to change my mind and accept your proposal.'

A look of astonishment crossed his face, and for one lowering moment she thought frantically that perhaps he had never meant it at all, and that he had been relieved at her refusal, but then he sat up abruptly, dislodging the pillows, and causing the bedding to slide down past his waist. Kate realised to her confusion that in trying to avoid looking directly into his eyes her gaze had somehow or other become fixed on his body, and that moreover she was seeing rather more of that body than was safe, and that her senses were already reacting to the sight of the dark arrowing of hair bisecting his flat belly.

'Am I permitted to ask why?'

The question was curt, so much so that she couldn't bring herself to look directly at him. Her courage was faltering, and would have left her completely if he hadn't suddenly reached out and taken hold of her wrist, saying surprisingly huskily, 'Kate, if you don't stop looking at me like that, I'm afraid I'm liable to ignore all the preliminaries and make love to you right here and now, and since I suspect that you aren't equipped to safeguard yourself against the results of our lovemaking and I know damned well that I'm not . . .'

All the cautious, carefully prepared phrases left her and, almost stammering with tension and emotion, she opened her palm and showed him the small box she had brought with her.

'It's this,' she tried to explain. 'The ring.'

'The ring?' He looked perplexed and baffled. '*That* made you change your mind. But why? It's not particularly valuable. I had planned on buying you another . . .'

'It's valuable to me,' Kate told him fiercely. 'It's valuable to me because . . .' She shook her head, unable to go on. 'Do you still *want* to marry me?'

'Since I've wanted to marry you for the last twenty-odd years, I'm hardly likely to have changed my mind in two short hours, am I?' he said derisively, and then, as she raised her head and gave him a swift, startled look of dawning realisation, he said gruffly, 'Come here.'

The ring and its box dropped to the floor as he caught hold of her, pulling her into the curve of his body as he silenced her questions with the warm pressure of his mouth.

They had kissed before, with passion, with tenderness... with fierce, elemental desire and with shy, youthful ardour, but this was the first time she had recognised in the meeting of their lips a mutual acknowledgement of commitment.

Kate trembled beneath the powerful force of the kiss. Now there was no going back ... now she was committed, but she still hadn't told him how she felt.

She started to pull away from him, but he was reluctant to release her. She tried to speak, but the words were silenced by the pressure of his mouth, but at last, when she pushed against his chest, he let her go.

'What's wrong?' he asked her softly, reaching up to push the tumbled curls back off her face. 'Am I taking too much for granted? I want to make love with you, Kate, but if you'd prefer to wait...'

She shook her head quickly, too desperate to unburden herself to notice the quick flare of desire darkening his eyes.

'There's something I have to tell you——' she began, but Joss interrupted her.

'Later. We can talk later,' he said thickly. 'Right now, all I want to do is what I've been aching to do since this morning.'

Kate shuddered as she felt him lift her hair away from her throat and subject the tender skin to tiny, biting kisses that gradually became more intense, lingering, teasing, tasting, until her whole body was a mass of jangled nerve-endings.

'Do you know what I wanted to do this morning?' Joss muttered into her skin between kisses. 'I wanted to do this ... and this ...'

His hands pushed aside her robe and caressed her breasts through the fine cotton of her nightdress.

'And this ...' he moaned thickly, dropping his head and nuzzling the hard peak of her breast through the cotton.

Kate couldn't help it. She gave a sharp cry of anguished need, her hands falling to his shoulders and then lifting to hold his head, while her body, possessed of a will of its own, arched in soft provocation.

'Kate, Kate ... it's been so long ...' Sharp teeth ravaged her tender flesh, sending delicious spirals of excitement coiling through her. She hated the barrier of her nightdress coming between them, aching for the sensation of his mouth against her bare flesh. Her hands released him and lifted impatiently to her shoulder straps, every movement instinctive and blind as she was caught up in the furious flood of emotion-spawned desire.

'Yes ... yes, I know ...' The warm male voice whispering against her skin made soft pockets of pleasure explode inside her. She was whimpering deep in her throat, stifled, tormented sounds she couldn't even hear, but which Joss could.

His hands trembled as he removed her nightdress.

'Is it this you want, Kate?' he whispered thickly against her breast, circling its rigid peak with his tongue. 'This...' His mouth opened over the hard, pulsing flesh and drew slowly on it until she almost screamed with pleasure.

Heat burst from her pores, her skin gleaming in the light of the lamp. When Joss stroked his hands over her, her body was slick and moist.

'This morning you didn't want me to touch you because you were like this,' he reminded her roughly. She tried to focus on him, to control the rapid rise and fall of her breathing, the shudders that racked her body... the need that coiled so fiercely through her belly.

'You're a woman, Kate, not a doll,' he whispered caressingly. 'And I love the scent, the feel, the taste of you...'

It was his use of the verb love that did it, smashing down every barrier she could have erected against him, breaking down the reserve she had built up over the years, sending her achingly, wantonly into his arms, the caution of years swept away as she touched him, kissed him, loved him without caution or restraint.

Once before they had loved, but not like this. Then she had been too shy, too immature to give pleasure as well as receive it. Now everything that she had always known by instinct but never allowed expression welled up inside her.

It was only when he felt the sensual rake of her teeth against the hard flesh of his outer thigh that

Joss stopped her, his hand sliding tensely into her hair and lifting her head.

'Generous Kate, but there's no need,' he said hoarsely. In the shadows of the room hazel eyes searched grey.

'Yes, there is,' Kate told him huskily. '*I* have the need.' Her hand rested possessively against his inner thigh, her nails unconsciously digging into his flesh.

'Please,' she begged unsteadily.

She needed the security of knowing he would allow her this intimacy; not just because it was a physical expression of her love, but because it would prove to her that, even if he couldn't love, he cared enough for her not to reject her...enough to permit the freedom of his body.

'*Please!*' His voice broke into rough disbelief as he repeated her plea. 'Oh, Kate, if you only knew how many times during the years I've ached for...longed for your touch...your hands...your mouth...'

He gave a deep shudder as she stared at him in silence. 'How many times I've tried to drown out that need, that ache with someone else and found that there was no pleasure in the act; only a soul-destroying self-contempt. *I* should be the one begging *you*,' he told her rawly. 'But I felt...I thought...I dared not let myself believe you'd want such intimacies, never mind initiate them.'

'You've *wanted* me...' Kate breathed uncertainly, her eyes rounding with surprise and disbelief.

'*Wanted* you?' He gave a bitter laugh. 'What a very small, mundane word to use to describe my feelings, but yes, I suppose you could say I've *wanted* you.'

'And you still...want me?' She plucked nervously at the sheet with her free hand.

His eyebrows rose. 'Do you really need to ask?' he mocked. Kate flushed, dipping her head, because the evidence of his wanting pulsed fiercely and strongly in front of her eyes. Unable to stop herself, she reached out and touched him lightly.

'Kate...'

A rough warning note deepened his voice, and when she raised her head she saw that his eyes were almost black with emotion.

As she looked at him, it was as though a burden was suddenly lifted from her shoulders. She bent her head and pressed her mouth tenderly against his belly and then his thighs, and then said quietly, 'I love you.'

For a moment it was as though he was frozen, and then, suddenly and illuminatingly, he started to tremble. He closed his eyes, and then opened them again and demanded blankly, 'Say that again.'

'I love you,' Kate repeated shakily.

He sat up abruptly and pushed his hand into his hair.

'Kate, what are you trying to do to me?' he protested rawly. 'First you arouse me to the point where I'm out of my mind with need...where I've just about reached the point where I'm willing to take anything...anything you're prepared to give me, despite the fact that I've already told myself that unless I have your love nothing else is worth while, and then, when you've destroyed every shred of self-resolve I've got, you calmly tell me that you love me.'

Kate's mouth had fallen open. This was the very last response she had expected to receive.

'You don't mind, then?' she faltered uncertainly.

'*Mind?*' He almost roared the word at her. 'Are you mad? Oh, Kate!'

He took hold of her and kissed her so passionately, so ruthlessly, that she could hardly breathe, and then, as the first insistent storm of emotion softened, he kept on kissing her, touching her, stroking her, his fingers moving against her throat as he felt the reverberations of the small impatient sounds she was stifling.

It had been such a long time since she had last made love, and as he moved her, positioned her, she had a momentary qualm of self-doubt. What if she should disappoint him? He was an experienced man, after all, while she... It was so shaming to acknowledge that her experience was limited to what she had learned from him, but as he felt her constraint he asked her what was wrong, and she had to tell him, 'Mind?' he said softly. '*Mind* knowing that every smallest response, every tiny reaction belongs only to me? Mind knowing that no one else can make you feel like this?' He spread her hair out on the pillow and twined his fingers into it, holding her prisoner.

'Oh, Kate. Let me show you how much I mind.'

Her body remembered much that her brain had forgotten. It shivered tempestuously, anticipating the pleasure of that first thrust, softening, opening, welcoming the raw male power of him inside it; pulses, rhythms, pleasures she remembered only as dim pastel shadows suddenly leapt to brilliant flaring life.

How could she have forgotten this, and this...and this? she wondered as she moved eagerly with him, wrapping herself around him, calling out to him to pleasure her, to fulfil her, to make her flesh quicken.

And even afterwards, when the tight, coiling need had exploded into a delight beyond words, she was reluctant to let him go, tightening her muscles around him as he moved, whispering drowsily, 'No, stay...'

'Kate...' She heard the rough emotion in his voice, opened her eyes sleepily and snuggled closer to him.

'The last woman I made love to was my ex-wife,' he whispered against her ear. 'She left me in no doubt that she found the experience less than satisfying, and yet you...'

He smoothed her hair back off her face and added, 'You said you loved me, and yet before, you told me you couldn't marry without love. There's no need to pretend to an emotion you don't feel, you know.'

Kate snuggled in his arms so that she could look at him.

'I do love you. I meant that I couldn't marry you because you don't love me...'

'What? Kate, I know you suffer from a lack of self-confidence, but surely even you must have realised how I feel about you!'

'I knew you desired me...but I thought it was only nostalgia. Something that would fade very quickly. I didn't want to burden you with my feelings.'

'Kate, I've never stopped loving you. Never.'

As he moved his head, she saw the shimmer of emotional tears darkening his eyes. She raised her head and kissed him gently, her heart overflowing with love and happiness.

Exactly a year later to the day, Kate looked across their crowded, newly decorated drawing-room to where Joss was standing by the window, expertly cradling the small bundle that was their three-month-old son.

'What a lovely christening,' John's mother commented warmly to her, 'and little Joshua was so good.' She eyed Sophy and John wistfully.

'I know they're only being sensible in waiting to start their family, but I must say, having a new baby in the family makes me hope they don't wait too long. And you look marvellous, Kate.'

'I had a good pregnancy, despite Joss's attempts to wrap me in cotton wool, and of course Joshua isn't my first baby...'

As she spoke she looked over the heads of their guests to where her first 'baby' was standing laughing with her father, while her three-month-old brother curled his tiny starfish hand around her finger.

At first, when she'd realised she was pregnant, she had been worried about what Sophy would think; the poor girl had already had two severe shocks—discovering her father, and then their marriage—and to present her with a third seemed more than a little unfair, but Sophy had been delighted, even though she hadn't been able to resist teasing her.

She would have teased her a good deal more, Kate suspected, had she realised that she and Joss had deliberately picked this date for the christening because it had been exactly a year today that their second child had been conceived. Exactly a year today since she and Joss had discovered their love...or rediscovered it; and since then her life had been filled with such pleasure and happiness. She saw Joss looking at her, and smiled back at him, her heart thudding with excited expectation...a sensation more suited to a girl in her twenties than a woman...but now she had promised Joss to stop harping on about her age.

He was, after all, as he had pointed out to her, five years her senior, and if *he* could behave like a besotted new husband and father, then she could most certainly behave like an adoring new wife and mother.

And tonight, for the first time since Joshua's birth, they would be able to make love. A small, sensual smile curled her mouth, and Joss, who had moved across the room to join her, murmured provocatively, 'Careful, Mrs Bennett, or have you forgotten how we came to have this unexpected bundle of joy?'

Smiling maternally into the sleeping face of their son, Kate responded tongue-in-cheek.

'I'm not sure.' She lifted her lashes and gave him a mock-demure look. 'An only child can be a lonely child.'

Joss groaned. 'Don't you dare. I was worried enough about you with this one.'

'Completely unnecessary,' Kate told him, rising up on tiptoe to kiss his jaw. 'There was nothing to worry about,' she told him seriously. 'These days women are having babies, and first babies at that, in their early forties, and I *am* only thirty-eight ...'

Their guests lifted their heads when Joss burst out laughing. Joshua opened his eyes and glowered protestingly at his father, and Kate, expertly scooping the baby out of her husband's arms, laughed with him as he bent his head and whispered teasingly, 'I see, now you're *only* thirty-eight ... What happened to being thirty-seven and ancient?'

'You did,' Kate told him lovingly.

Joss looked from his wife to his son, and then back again, and replied musingly, 'Mmm. Well, perhaps you're right. An only child *can* be lonely...'

'What are you two plotting?' Sophy demanded mock-severely, coming to join them, not understanding the laughter they exchanged as they refused to tell her.

Harlequin Presents®

Coming Next Month

Available in January wherever paperback books are sold, or through
Harlequin Reader Service:

In the U.S.
901 Fuhrmann Blvd.
P.O. Box 1397
Buffalo, N.Y. 14240-1397

In Canada
P.O. Box 603
Fort Erie, Ontario
L2A 5X3

Take 4 bestselling love stories FREE

Plus get a FREE surprise gift!

**Harlequin romances are now available in stores
at these convenient times each month.**

Harlequin Presents **Harlequin American Romance** **Harlequin Historical** **Harlequin Intrigue**	These series will be in stores on the 4th of every month.
Harlequin Romance **Harlequin Temptation** **Harlequin Superromance** **Harlequin Regency Romance**	New titles for these series will be in stores on the 16th of every month.

We hope this new schedule is convenient for you. With
only two trips each month to your local bookseller, you
will always be sure not to miss any of your favorite
authors!

Happy reading!

Please note there may be slight variations in on-sale dates
in your area due to differences in shipping and handling.

HDATES